COUSINS

STUCK IN THE MIDDLE

Other Apple paperbacks
by Colleen O'Shaughnessy McKenna

Mother Murphy
The Truth About Sixth Grade
Murphy's Island
Merry Christmas, Miss McConnell!
Fifth Grade: Here Comes Trouble
Eenie, Meanie, Murphy, No!
Fourth Grade Is a Jinx
Too Many Murphys

And the first COUSINS book
Not Quite Sisters

STUCK IN THE MIDDLE

Colleen O'Shaughnessy McKenna

SCHOLASTIC INC.
New York Toronto London Auckland Sydney

ISBN 0-590-49429-5

12 11 10 9 8 7 6 5 4 3 2 3 4 5 6 7 8/9

Printed in the U.S.A. 40

First Scholastic printing, August 1993

Dedicated with love and best wishes to my sister Michelle in celebration of her college graduation, May 1993 — a true artist!

COUSINS

STUCK IN THE MIDDLE

1

"Aren't you *sooooooo* excited to be turning thirteen, Callie?" asked Lindsay. She's my cousin and very best friend in the world.

"I thought I was, but look at this closet, Lins!" I swung open both doors and stood back. "How does my mom expect me to turn *thirteen* wearing any of these clothes?" I held out a pink checked sundress with a full pleated skirt. "I had my picture taken back in the fifth grade wearing this."

"And you looked real cute in it, too. Do you still have the matching pink socks with the lace?" laughed Lindsay.

"Very funny. My whole wardrobe looks like it came from the Mother Goose Boutique!" I cried, waving a sailor dress with a large red bow in her face.

Lindsay shrugged. "I'll take anything you don't want. I'm only starting sixth grade. Anything works for me!"

I sifted through the rest of the clothes, groaning

and shaking my head. I was beginning to think my mother didn't want me to grow up. "I need to go shopping before the party on Saturday."

"I like your clothes," said Lindsay. She usually likes everything about me. Which proves she has very good taste, of course.

I flopped down on the bed next to her. "Oh, take them, Lins, take them all. How can I start the seventh grade dressed as a four-year-old? I asked my mom a zillion times to please buy me a new wardrobe before school starts."

"She should take you," Lindsay agreed. "You're an only child, poor baby. It's your job to be spoiled. In all the old movies, couples with only one child let them have whatever they wanted."

"My parents aren't going to the right movies then." I rolled over on my stomach and sighed. "Besides, Lins, haven't you noticed that it's impossible to be spoiled in this house? Who unloads the dishwasher every night? Me! Who takes out the trash? Me!"

Lindsay laughed and threw her arm around me. "Oh, you poor little darling."

I smiled back. "I bet if we had a dog, I'd be the one walking it around the block in the pouring rain."

Lindsay shook her head and hopped off the bed. "Face it, cuz, you have one tough life."

"Yeah." I started to laugh. "My mom said I could ask as many kids as I wanted to the party."

"Great." Lindsay stuck her head in my closet and started going through my clothes. "Remind your mom how important it is to look positively cool for your birthday party on Saturday."

"Hey, Lins. My mom's the oldest of seven, remember? She says all you really need for a birthday party is a cake and lots of balloons."

"Well, dar-link cousin, that was back in the olden days. Besides, Scott Randel is coming to your party! Everything has to be first class." Lindsay took an armload of clothes and draped them on the back of a chair. "Gee, thanks for the clothes, Callie. I think I'll wear this yellow sundress to your party."

"Lindsay!" I scrambled off the bed. "What are you doing? I was only joking. You can't take my clothes."

Lindsay frowned and slumped against the closet door. "Wow, talk about backing out of a deal. These clothes would look great on me."

I laughed. "Sorry, but if you take my clothes, I'll be at my party wearing nothing but a smile."

Lindsay laughed. "A perfect birthday outfit for you, Callie. Wrinkle-free."

"Yeah, sure. Scott Randel and his band of loonies would laugh me off this planet." As I stood in front of her mirror, I sucked in my stomach. "Hey, Lins, do I look older than I did at the beginning of summer vacation?"

Lindsay squinted one eye and studied me. Since

we were only eleven months apart, and very best friends, she would give an honest answer.

"Hmmmm, do you look older?" repeated Lindsay. "Interesting question. Hmmmmmm. Let me see. Turn around, lady."

I held out my arms and spun around. Then I yanked the elastic from my five-hundred-pound, thick red hair. "Tell me the truth."

Lindsay stared hard. She opened her eyes wide, then narrowed them. Finally she frowned and shook her head. "No."

"No?"

Lindsay shook her head. "No. My professional, best friend-slash-best cousin opinion is you look *exactly* the same, Callie. Except maybe you grew an inch or two."

I clapped my hands. "Yes! Yes! An inch or two is all I needed. Lins, that's great!"

"Wellllll, maybe not so great, Callie. Your inches aren't in the right places." Lindsay giggled. "I think they're in your feet. Maybe your arms are a little longer."

"What?" I tried to frown, but ended up laughing as I grabbed the clothes from the chair and hung them back in the closet. "Yeah, well, your curves aren't stopping traffic, either."

"I know." Lindsay grabbed a handful of blonde hair and piled it on top of her head. "But I'm younger, dar-link. Besides, I don't have competition like MaryBeth. It's hard to believe you two are the same age. I mean, holy cow, did you see her since she got back from vacation? I don't know where she went, but she's even prettier, and she was wearing a tiny two-piece at the community pool. The lifeguard dropped his whistle when she walked by. Whatever you do, don't stand next to her at your party."

"Thanks, Lindsay." I tugged on her ponytail. "Maybe I'll ask everyone to dress in potato sacks so we'll all look alike."

"Even then, MaryBeth would be a fancy, Grade A potato, and we would be garden spuds." Lindsay laughed. "The worst part is, MaryBeth is so nice you can't even dislike her."

"I know. She can't help it she's so pretty and has the perfect figure."

Lindsay picked up her sweatshirt. "Yeah, and here you are, Miss Birthday Girl, without any figure."

"Thanks a lot, Lindsay!" I tossed my stuffed cat at her.

Lindsay ducked and giggled. "Hey, it's not your fault. Besides, school doesn't start for another month. There's still time for your hormones to kick in. Maybe they're stuck."

"Yeah, I'll do a couple hundred jumping jacks to unstick them."

"I'd better get going." Lindsay opened the bedroom door and paused. "Listen, Callie. Anything can happen. I bet you'll be the type to blossom overnight. It happens all the time in the movies. I saw this old movie once where this girl was just an ugly duckling kind of person. Then, her poor family sent her to pick peaches on this huge plantation. She ate lots of peaches and got healthy-looking, spent weeks in the sun and got a great tan, brushed her hair out of her braids, and turned beautiful. The next thing she knew, the owner of the plantation galloped by on his white horse and asked her to marry him."

I laughed. Lindsay was always learning things from watching old movies. "Is there a message here, Lindsay?"

"Yeah, there is. Don't worry. You won't always look so, well, ordinary."

"What?"

"Not bad ordinary. Just, like, well . . . like all the rest of us. And then there are girls like MaryBeth and Luisa who are fancy-looking real early in life."

I nodded. Lindsay was probably right. I looked like everyone's sister or cousin. Besides, I never really thought about how I looked before. I looked like me, Callie Gaitlin.

"Besides, if you wear big shirts no one will even notice you still have your sixth-grade body."

"Lindsay!" The trouble with asking for the truth from Lindsay was, that's what you got.

"Hey, just a suggestion, lady," giggled Lindsay. "Keep your world famous temper in."

"Thanks for the pep talk. Want to go to the pool after lunch? I want to work on my tan for my birthday."

"Sure. You could use another dozen freckles," laughed Lindsay. "There's an empty spot near your chin."

"At least I'll have something new for my party."

"Ask your mom to take you shopping one more time. Tell her you have to make a dramatic switch before Saturday."

"Okay. I'll tell her you're worried about my image."

"I am. I'm trying to help you." Lindsay grinned and snapped her fingers. "That's it!"

"That's what?"

"I'll be your coach. I'll teach you everything you need to know to turn thirteen."

I flopped back on the bed. "Oh, brother. Thanks, but, no thanks!"

"It will be so much fun." Lindsay plopped down on the bed next to me. "Think of it, Callie. I'll coach your summer switch. No one will recognize you by the time you start seventh grade."

I sat up and frowned. "I don't need a coach, Lins. I mean, turning thirteen is not a big deal."

"But!" Lindsay held up one finger. "It could be."

"You're nuts, Lindsay."

"Call me Coach."

"You're nuts, Coach."

As soon as Lindsay raced down the stairs, I

faced the mirror again. Maybe I did need a coach. I had huge feet, my hair was too red, and all five foot six of me was too skinny to be called anything but ordinary. The only thing about me that attracted attention was my temper. Most people encouraged me to keep it hidden. It only had one speed: *full steam ahead.*

Which left what?

An ugly duckling?

"Oh, phooey, anyway," I muttered, turning my back on the mirror. "Who cares?" Lindsay would soon get tired of trying to coach me into a dazzling teenager. It wouldn't work. Even if I could talk my mom into taking me to the Sweetwater Mall, no store in Texas sold what I needed.

2

Three hours later, Coach Lindsay came by with my other cousin, Jessica, so we could walk over to the community pool. With both of them talking a mile a minute on either side of me, my ears were vibrating with stereo waves. I didn't mind a bit. In fact, it was hard to believe that my cousin Jessica had arrived in Sweetwater a few weeks before, refusing to speak to anyone at all. That had been a little scary.

"So, before we get started, let me jot down a few things," announced Lindsay.

Lindsay actually had a notebook with her. She wrote down that I was finally wearing a nice new two-piece bathing suit, and was planning to bring a *Little Mermaid* towel.

"Sorry, Callie, but you've got to bring another towel," Lindsay informed me. She snapped closed her notebook and rammed it into her swim bag.

"What?" I sniffed my towel. No one would notice that it had been wadded up in the bottom of my closet for two days.

Lindsay sighed and pointed to Ariel. "The fish chick is a dead giveaway that you're twelve."

"I am twelve." Besides, I loved my mermaid towel.

"Callie, Callie, Callie," sighed Lindsay. She hopped up on the kitchen counter. "I am your coach, right?"

"Right."

"And my job is to get you ready to turn thirteen, right?"

"Right."

Lindsay held out both arms and smiled. "So, trust me, then, cuz. Ditch the towel. Go get one of your mom's good company towels. Maybe one with a monogram."

"My mom only uses them when company comes!"

Lindsay growled, I swear she did. "Go get a new towel, Callie. And bring some lip gloss. Your lips are looking very twelvish." Lindsay rummished around in her swim bag and pulled out her notebook. "I'll make a note to buy you some strawberry-scented lip gloss. It's very grown-up to have lips that smell like fruit."

Jessica laughed out loud. "You are too much, Lindsay."

"Go ahead and laugh," muttered Lindsay, already scribbling something else in her notebook.

"Just wait until we turn thirteen, Jessica. When I get finished with Callie, I'll have all the kinks worked out."

"I'm a kink?" I tossed my mermaid towel in the laundry room and grabbed a navy-blue one from the dryer. My mother would kill me if I got suntan lotion on her good towels.

"Not a kink, but . . ." Lindsay paused to frown at my navy towel. "But, you are a little stubborn, Callie. And your temper only has one speed . . . red-hot! No offense, but those things might slow you down a little."

Jessica opened the pantry and tossed me a bag of pretzels. "You're going to need to keep your strength up, Callie. We'd better bring these."

"Toss me the corn curls, too," I called out.

Lindsay flew to the pantry, slamming it shut so fast, Jessica jumped back. "No corn curls! Bring an apple, or a quart of milk. You've got to eat food that the models eat from now on."

"Lindsay!" I drummed my nails against the table. The back of my neck was beginning to prickle, a sure sign that my temper was up on all fours. "I am not trying out for the swimsuit issue of *Sports Illustrated.* I am just turning thirteen!"

Lindsay rolled her eyes. "Just turning thirteen, she says."

"But, she is just turning thirteen," pointed out Jessica. She looked at me and we both started to laugh.

Lindsay flipped open her notebook and wrote faster than ever.

I tried to see what she was writing. I knew it wasn't good.

"I am writing that you are being very uncooperative," Lindsay said slowly. She looked pretty upset.

"We were only kidding, Lins," said Jessica. She got upset whenever anyone else was upset.

I nudged Lindsay. "Okay, I'll bring an apple. Maybe even a grapefruit."

Lindsay looked up and smiled.

"You're nice to be so worried about me," I said. I opened the pantry and grabbed a box of oatmeal. "Here," I said, thumping it down on the counter. "I'll eat a bowl of this every morning."

Lindsay laughed. "With chopped-up prunes, Callie."

"And a salad on the side," added Jessica.

We joked all the way to the pool. I knew how lucky I was to have such fun cousins. Being the oldest was the hardest job, so I decided to relax and let them both take care of me for a while.

We spread our towels out by the lifeguard's chair. This was the best spot for people watching since all the high school girls walked by the guard's chair a zillion times a day.

I opened my book and rolled over on my stomach.

"Callie!"

I glanced up. Coach looked worried. She was holding her notebook.

"You can't start reading the moment you get to the pool," corrected Lindsay. "Sit up for a while, look around. Check out who's here. Try to look thirteen!"

"But I love this book. One chapter, okay?"

Lindsay groaned. She closed her eyes and folded her notebook in half. "Pleeeeeeeassssse, don't argue with me."

Jessica pretended she was scratching her nose, but I could tell she was trying hard not to laugh.

"Okay, okay." I set down my book and sat up. I cleaned my sunglasses. Only twelve-year-olds wore smudgy lenses.

"That's better," said Lindsay. She set down her notebook and smiled.

"Gosh, did you see MaryBeth's dive?" I asked.

"Okay, okay, so MaryBeth looks great in a tank suit and she can do a back flip off the high dive," Lindsay said slowly, squirting a long thin stream of suntan lotion down her leg. "The important question is, can the girl name all eight planets of the solar system?"

"Nine planets, Lins," I laughed. "You're forgetting your birthplace, Mars."

"Actually, scientists think there are ten planets," added Jessica. "Hey, give me back my lotion before you use it all up, Lindsay. I just bought it." Lindsay tossed the tube of lotion and shoved her sunglasses up on her nose. "Oh, dar-links. What a great day. The sun is so high, the water so cold. Our training program is off to a great start."

"I think you've been in the sun too long, Lindsay," I laughed. "You're not making sense and your nose is peeling."

Lindsay sat up and rubbed her nose. "Well, at least it isn't your nose, Callie. I mean, you are the birthday girl."

"Did you ask everyone to your party, Callie?" asked Jessica.

I shook my head. "I need to invite a few more boys. We have twelve girls coming and only four boys. Everyone fun is at basketball camp. Except Scott, and he doesn't count."

Lindsay yanked off her sunglasses and coughed. "Excuse me, but did you say that Scott doesn't *count?* Are you nuts? Scott Randel is so cute, he is the only one who *should* count."

I made a face, hoping she wasn't going to write that down in her notebook. I lay back down on my towel. I really wanted to get back to my book. "Oh, Lindsay, when are you going to realize that Scott Randel is just another boy living in Sweetwater, Texas?"

Lindsay laughed. "I guess when he stops walking around with curly blond hair and long eyelashes, flashing that terrific smile."

Jessica giggled. "He does have nice teeth."

"He has nice everything," sighed Lindsay. "All the boys in my grade still smell like peanut butter most of the time."

I stabbed Lindsay in the back with my toe. "I love peanut butter. Am I still allowed to eat that?"

"Probably not. Too much fat."

"I bet Scott eats whatever he wants." I picked up my book again. Maybe Lindsay was so busy dreaming about Scott, she wouldn't notice.

"Scott really is very nice," Jessica added fairly.

"So are Billy Beepers and Walter Poplar," I pointed out.

Lindsay buried her face in her towel and groaned. "Oh, stop. Billy paints his nails and Walter smells like dirty socks."

"But they are very nice," I laughed. "Very dependable."

"So is our mailman, but who cares?" sighed Jessica. "Scott is special!"

"Oh, my gosh, speak of the devil," giggled Lindsay. She tossed her towel to the right and waved. "Hi, Scott."

Lindsay reached over and snatched my book.

"Hey, guys," said Scott. His hand shot up in a brief salute as he walked by. "See you Saturday, Callie. Do you feel another year older?"

"I feel fine," I told him. "See ya."

When Scott turned the corner and walked into the rest room, Lindsay reached over and pinched me.

"Yeow!" I cried. You never knew what Lindsay was going to do. It was dangerous sitting next to her. "What was that for?"

"For acting like . . . like one of the guys!" sputtered Lindsay.

"I was acting like myself." I bent down and rubbed my leg. It was already turning red. Lindsay had a healthy temper herself.

"Callie, if someone as cute as Scott mentions your birthday, you should start talking about the party. How much fun we're going to have. Maybe flirt a little and say you can't believe you're finally a teenager."

"What are you talking about?" I asked. Half the time, I never knew *what* Lindsay was talking about. She was usually talking about two or three different things at the same time.

"MaryBeth would have stood up and wrapped her cute little towel around her hips and said, 'Oh, Scott, I'm just scared to death to finally be a teenager and start junior high.' " Lindsay poked me. "And then Scott would have spent the next ten minutes telling you that he's thirteen and it's cool and if you're scared about junior high, he'll walk you to every class."

I leaned over and gave Lindsay a little pinch back. "Oh, yeah, well, I can't wrap *my* cute little towel around me because you made me leave it at home. And I refuse to pretend to be scared about turning thirteen or going to junior high."

"Aren't you scared?" asked Jessica. She had just moved down from Pittsburgh and everyone knew she was scared to death about starting a new school. Luckily, Lindsay would be with her.

"No, I'm not scared," I said. "I still look and feel exactly like a twelve-year-old. Nothing has changed. School will still be school. Period." My voice had climbed to a shrill squeak. Maybe I was scared.

Lindsay lowered her sunglasses and peered at me. "All seventh-graders are afraid to start junior high, Callie. It's a tradition."

"I'm not." I wondered if telling the same lie counted twice with God.

"Ha!" said Lindsay. She pulled a baseball cap down low on her forehead. "And double ha!"

"Don't double ha me, Lins. What do you mean?" I wanted to know.

"If someone as perfect as MaryBeth is scared to be starting the seventh grade, then . . ."

"Then what?" I could almost smell an insult.

Lindsay pushed up her cap. "Then someone like you has to be scared, or has to be lying."

"Lindsay!" said Jessica. "Callie doesn't have to be scared."

I felt like hugging Jessica. It was nice to know at least one cousin was on my side.

"Well, then," said Lindsay, grabbing the suntan

lotion and regreasing her entire arm. She was acting as if she was the one who bought the lotion in the first place.

"Well, then, what?" I grabbed the lotion back and gave it to Jessica.

"Then show me you're not scared by walking over there and asking Scott to help you set up for your party. Believe me, Callie, you need to be in the cool group starting junior high, or you might end up being a big nobody. Thirteen-year-olds always have boys for their good friends. Then, when they're sixteen, they fall in love."

"Are you crazy, Lindsay?" I wanted to pick her up and toss her in the pool. "I don't need any help setting up for the party. How hard is it to carry a bowl of pretzels out to my patio?"

"Set up a volleyball net. Set up a scavenger hunt. Set up a dance floor." Lindsay was grinning from ear to ear. "Set up something!"

"Why?"

"Because asking a handsome boy for help is a very grown-up move. Even though you still look twelve, you've got to start *acting* thirteen. The sooner the better. I am your coach, after all. I'll be on my fifth notebook if you don't start helping me."

"Why are you such an expert anyway? Did you read some sort of dumb manual on what kids are *supposed* to do when they turn thirteen, Lindsay?"

"Yes, in a way," said Lindsay. "I watched a movie where a girl started college when she was only fifteen. Next, she fell in love with her twenty-one-year-old chemistry professor. Her friends said she was too young for him, so she asked him out to lunch to prove that age didn't matter. She wanted to show everyone she could handle it. It was a very fancy restaurant, so this girl wore a hat and little white gloves."

"What?" I don't know where Lindsay finds all these strange movies to watch. She must be hooked up to a cable station from Mars.

"What happened?" asked Jessica. She looked interested, as if she wished she had seen the movie, too.

Lindsay grinned. "Well, things were fine at first, but then this girl got all mixed up remembering which fork to use and then she started cutting her steak with a butter knife, and after lunch she ordered chocolate milk instead of coffee . . . and she blew it and finally confessed she was only fifteen! The same thing could happen to you, Callie, unless you listen to me."

I buried my head under my towel. Too bad I was the oldest cousin. Too bad I didn't have a ninth-grader in the family who could show me the ropes. I sure wasn't going to learn a thing about being a teenager from Lindsay or Jessica.

"Now if only this girl had taken the time to learn about being twenty-one, she may have been able to fool this professor. But she didn't do her homework, so she left college and got a job collecting tolls on the New Jersey Turnpike." Jessica was watching me. She wasn't really used to Lindsay and me, yet, full-time. Before her move to Sweetwater, she had only seen us on holidays.

"Well, I certainly don't want people throwing quarters at me all day, Lindsay," I said, surprising myself as I hopped to my feet. "So, if it will prove something to you, Lindsay, then I'll ask Scott to pleassssse help me set up the volleyball net for my party." The whole idea was so stupid. I had been setting up the net since I was ten. All by myself. And Scott couldn't teach me a thing about being thirteen. I liked the kid fine. But I didn't have a huge crush on him like thousands of other girls in town. I had known Scott Randel since we were both two and going to the same Sunday school camp. But to keep Lindsay happy and Jessica reassured, I would walk over and ask him for his thirteen-year-old help. Jeez, what some cousins won't do to keep peace.

"Way to go," cheered Lindsay, giving me a drumroll with her flip-flops. "That's my girl!"

I grinned back, deciding to try out my new thirteen-year-old walk. I tossed my red hair over one shoulder and tried to remember how MaryBeth managed to sway to the left and right as she walked. Left. Right. Left. Right. Okaaaay!

I was just beginning to get the rhythm of it as

I rounded the water fountain and headed for the snack bar. Scott and his friends were walking toward me. I fluffed up my hair with my left hand and glanced back at Lindsay and Jessica to catch their reaction. Whoa, talk about a fast learner! I was a natural.

I was still fluffing, still looking over my shoulder, when I started swaying left, when I should have swayed right. The next thing I knew, I was flying over a lawn chair, soaring straight through the air toward a horrified Scott Randel.

3

"What are you, *crazy*?" sputtered Scott. He pushed me off and stood up. "Tryouts for the football team are next month, Callie!"

"Yo! What a tackle!" joked Brad. "A flag was dropped for clipping, though."

Scott grinned as everyone started to laugh. I wasn't laughing. I was sure Lindsay was writing in her notebook, and my leg was killing me. I was positive my forehead was grass-stained. "Sorry, Scott," I managed to say. "I guess I didn't see you."

"Time to get your eyes checked, Callie, if you can't see Scott. He's a pretty big target to miss," giggled MaryBeth. She was leaning against the guard's room, with her pale pink towel wrapped neatly around her hips. The girl did not seem to need any tutoring in acting thirteen.

"You okay, Callie?" asked Scott. He tossed me a towel. "Your forehead's green."

I buried my face in the towel, wishing I could

keep it there forever. Kids were still laughing, teasing Scott about being tackled by a girl. Too bad I wasn't still ten. I would have tackled Brad and Jack both.

"Tackled by our own Red Baron!" hooted Jack. "The great Scott Randel, brought down by a ninety-pound girl."

I yanked down the towel and glared at Jack. "That's ten more pounds than *you* weigh, Jack."

Jack pretended to be shocked, but he grinned down at me. "You'd better be nice or I won't come to your party."

Scott grabbed his towel back. "Yeah, the big thirteen. Is your mom going to rent that clown?"

"That was six years ago, Scott," I replied in an icy tone. Chuckles the clown had actually been pretty funny. Much funnier than the clowns who surrounded me at the pool.

"I'll bring some tapes," offered Jack.

"Thanks. Can I talk to you, Scott?" I asked.

"Yeah, let's go sit down. I think you broke my leg."

"Ha-ha," I mumbled as I followed him back across the grass. I followed Scott through the maze of green and yellow lawn chairs, back to the fence, which was usually saved for the junior high kids. I glanced around nervously, wondering if any eighth-grader was about to pop out and tell us to scram.

"Are you going out for football?" I asked. I loved

going to the junior high football games. Everyone in town brought a lawn chair to watch.

"Yeah. But I don't know if I'll make the team. I've been eating like a horse all summer, but I've only grown two inches."

I glanced down at my swimsuit. I could have used two inches this summer.

"You're a good player," I said fairly. "And you're fast. Brad's huge but slow."

Scott grinned. "Thanks, but being good in the sixth grade isn't the same as being good in the seventh. Things change."

I studied Scott's face, wondering if he was trying to tell me he was nervous about junior high, too. Maybe he wanted me to confess. Did boys worry about the same things girls did?

"But it doesn't have to be a bad change. I mean, we'll still know lots of the same kids," I said. "We can be friends with them."

"I know that. I'm not worried about making friends. I'm worried about getting to class on time and making the football team."

"Me, too."

"What?" Scott started coughing. "Are you going out for the team?

My face flooded red. "No. I meant being on time for class."

"I might wear Rollerblades the first day."

I stood up, glancing over at Lindsay who was

still watching me. "Well, I guess we have to get through the rest of the summer first. I hope my mom doesn't plan anything corny for my party."

"Moms usually do."

I stood up to leave, then remembered my mission. I didn't want Lindsay throwing her notebook at me if I came back empty-handed. "Hey, Scott. I want to set up the volleyball net on Saturday."

Scott nodded, closing his eyes and stretching out in his chair. After a minute, he opened one eye and stared at me. "So, what are you waiting for? My permission? Go ahead, Callie. Live dangerously, set up that net."

"Very funny," I said. I laughed loudly anyway, since Lindsay and Jessica were watching me. Maybe Lindsay would give me an extra point for being funny with a boy. "Actually, Scott, I hate to be a pain, but do you think you could come early, maybe six-thirty, and help me set up the net?"

Scott looked puzzled. I felt stupid. I knew how to change a flat tire; of course I could set up a volleyball net.

"Sure. If you want me to."

"Thanks, 'cause I know I'll be real busy getting all the food ready and stuff like that."

Scott started to grin. "Food? Okay. Have tons of it because I have to grow another two inches before school starts."

You and me both, I thought.

"Thanks, Scott. I'll see you around six-thirty then."

"Okay. I'll probably bring Garret, if that's okay."

"Sure." Who was Garret, a chaperone?

As soon as I got within grabbing distance, Lindsay and Jessica grabbed me. "You're really brave, Callie," they declared proudly. Lindsay had tears in her eyes, I swear.

"He's coming at six-thirty." I tried to sound casual.

"You are so terrrrribly grown-up," said Lindsay.

I smiled and let them lead me over to the snack bar for a celebration soda.

"Fries, too, Coach?" I asked. "Since I was so brave?"

"Just this once," Lindsay said sternly. "And Jessica and I will help you eat them."

We got our order and walked back out into the bright sunlight.

"Hi, guys!" said MaryBeth. She and Luisa waved and scooted over to make room for us. "Sit here."

I slid down next to MaryBeth, glancing at her fresh fruit platter.

"All set for your party, Callie?" MaryBeth asked.

"Pretty much so. There isn't that much to do." I pushed my platter of fries closer. "Want some?"

MaryBeth made a face and shook her head. "No, thanks. I've already gained five pounds this summer."

Lindsay choked on her Coke. We both knew how we'd love to trade those five pounds with her.

"Callie's party will be so much fun," gushed Lindsay, daintily dipping her fry in a glob of bright yellow mustard. "Scott Randel is coming over early to help Callie. He insisted."

"What?" MaryBeth held her fork in midair. "Scott is coming early?"

Lindsay nodded. "Yes. Isn't that sweet of him? He doesn't want Callie getting worn out. What a guy!"

Luisa nudged MaryBeth with her elbow. "What a creep!"

I dropped my French fry. Who was the creep? Me?

"Scott is such a flirt," said MaryBeth. She pushed her plate away and crossed her arms. "Boys!"

"What's wrong?" I asked.

MaryBeth just looked across the pool, so Luisa filled in the facts. "Scott's the creep. He called MaryBeth last night and asked her to walk over to your party with him. Now he's telling you he'll come early and be with you."

I dropped my fry. "Well, he's not really coming to be *with* me. I mean, he's just setting up the volleyball net, and . . ."

Lindsay smiled and patted MaryBeth on the hand. "Scott loves parties. He's just trying to help. Callie and Scott go *waaaay* back."

I kicked Lindsay under the table. "It won't take long, MaryBeth. Scott is bringing a friend, too. Some kid named Garret."

"Garret Novak?" MaryBeth grinned. "Whoa, I heard about that kid from Judy Lee. You should try to get him to stay for your party, Callie. I heard he was the best-looking boy in Sweetwater."

"Nooooooo!" Lindsay held her French fry in midair. "Cuter than Scott?"

MaryBeth giggled. "Different cuter." She leaned forward and started to whisper. "His name is Garret Novak and Judy Lee says he looks sixteen or seventeen. His hair is black, and his eyes are so blue, he must wear contacts."

"He doesn't," Luisa said quickly. "Lynna saw him at the tennis courts yesterday and she asked him."

"She *asked* him?" MaryBeth looked shocked. "That wasn't very cool."

"Why?" I wanted to know. It wasn't as if she asked him what kind of deodorant he wears.

MaryBeth shrugged. "I just think you have to be more subtle in the seventh grade. Sure, you want to find out things, but you don't just . . . ASK!"

Lindsay nodded. "Yeah, remember that, Callie."

"What?"

Lindsay leaned closer to MaryBeth. "Truthfully, Callie asked Scott to come and help her set up the volleyball net, but that was before she knew that she was supposed to be subtle."

"What?" MaryBeth's cheeks were getting pink. "You *asked* Scott?"

I nodded, then shook my head, and finally settled on a shrug. "Well, yeah. I mean, I didn't know you had dibs on him or anything. He's just a friend."

Luisa nudged MaryBeth. "He's MaryBeth's friend, too."

"I thought he was," muttered MaryBeth. She shook back her hair and sighed. "Boys can be so rude. Go ahead and ask him to mow your lawn. I don't care."

"Can't he be everyone's friend?" asked Lindsay. She clapped her hand over her mouth. "I mean, sorry for asking, but . . ."

MaryBeth stood up and adjusted her towel. "Scott Randel can be friends with every girl in Sweetwater if he wants. In fact, I think I'm going to tell him right now that he doesn't have to walk me to your party. I am a big girl and I can walk myself over."

"MaryBeth, he doesn't have to help me with the net. It's not a big deal." Gosh, if turning thirteen was going to cause so much trouble, I'd stay twelve for the rest of my life. "Are you mad at me, MaryBeth?"

"No, you didn't know," said MaryBeth. "Besides, as my mother always says, 'There are plenty of fish in the sea!' "

Luisa stood up and glared across the pool at Scott. "And Scott Randel might just find himself getting replaced by a catch like Garret Novak anyway."

"MaryBeth, don't be mad at him. I mean, I'm the one who asked him to come early." I bit my lip, wondering how I could get out of this without looking too stupid. "I'll tell him not to come early. My dad can set up the net."

"I'll set it up," offered Jessica. She was nervous now, eating her French fries so fast she was liable to snap off a fingertip.

MaryBeth picked up her fruit plate and tossed it into the trash can. "It's not your fault, Callie. But it's time someone taught Mr. Randel a lesson in manners."

"Yeah," added Luisa. "Grown-up manners."

Both girls marched off toward the fence.

"Phew, poor Scott," muttered Lindsay. "He won't even know what hit him."

I grabbed my plate and pitched it as I flew past the trash can. Out of the corner of my eye I saw

MaryBeth and Luisa turn by the guard's room. In another second, they would be yelling at Scott in front of all of his friends. Then Scott would shout that he didn't want to set up my volleyball net in the first place. Soon everyone would be yelling and screaming. It wouldn't take long. Just long enough for my party plans to take a fatal nosedive.

4

MaryBeth must not have yelled at Scott too much, because five minutes later they were dunking each other in the pool and laughing a lot.

"You were lucky this time, Callie," declared Lindsay as she scribbled in her notebook. "Next time you ask a boy to help you do something, make sure he didn't already promise another girl, especially MaryBeth, that he would be helping her."

"Hey, I never wanted to ask Scott to help me in the first place," I sputtered. "That was your idea, Coach!"

Lindsay glared at me above her notebook. "The idea was a good one, Callie. But next time, be sure and — "

"There won't be a next time," I muttered. "I won't ask a boy to help me do another thing."

"Let's just go home," suggested Jessica. "It's getting cloudy, anyway."

"Great idea," said Lindsay. "I say we go home

and ask Callie's mom to let her go to the mall and pick out a new birthday outfit."

"My mom will say no," I answered.

"Your mom already said yes," Lindsay replied with a smirk. "As your wonderful coach, I already had my mom suggest the idea this morning and your mom said it was okay."

I was shocked. "My mom said okay?"

Lindsay made a small bow. "Yes. My mom said she would drive both ways and make sure you didn't spend too much money."

I started to think that having Lindsay for a coach wasn't such a bad idea after all. I was getting a new outfit out of it.

Right before we left for the mall I called Scott and told him to forget about coming early to my party to help. I convinced him that I loved volleyball so much, I came home from swimming and set up the net myself. I didn't want to be the one to come between Scott and MaryBeth.

I couldn't believe how well things were going. I had nothing to worry about. No one was mad at me, and I wouldn't have to wear a little sunsuit with rabbits embroidered on it to my party.

Lindsay's mom drove us to the Sweetwater Mall and said she would meet us in front of JC Penney's in four hours. That was plenty of time for a movie and shopping.

We had a lot of fun at the movie. Lindsay was glued to the end of her seat, mouth half open, and grinning: the way she gets when she watches good movies. Jessica and I went through a tub of buttered popcorn and all three of us cried at the end.

"Do you think we'll still cry at movies when we're on a date?" asked Jessica.

"If it's sad we will," I answered.

"You can't, ladies," warned Lindsay. "You can't cry on dates. Boys will get nervous and never ask you out again."

"Oh, you're crazy. They will, too." I nudged Lindsay with my elbow. "I've seen girls on dates crying in movies before."

Lindsay shook her head. "Then they were engaged girls, Callie. It's okay to cry at movies if you're engaged, married, or, or . . . just old. Otherwise, it's not cool."

Jessica and I laughed. Lindsay thought she knew every single rule about life. She probably got her facts off the backs of cereal boxes.

"Oh, my gosh." Lindsay grabbed my arm and squeezed. "Speaking of dates, girls! Look who's here."

Scott Randel was standing in the lobby of the movie theater with someone so handsome, it had to be Garret Novak.

"Holy moley, Scott is adorable, but that kid he's with is gorgeous!" Lindsay cried.

"He can't be thirteen," I whispered. "He has to be sixteen, maybe twenty-three."

"Too bad he's not twelve," whispered Lindsay.

Jessica nodded. "Some boys just look old faster. Up in Pittsburgh there were some boys living next door who were only thirteen and fourteen, and they already shaved."

"No," groaned Lindsay. "Whoa. I've never talked to a boy who smelled like after-shave lotion. Boy, I would be a nervous wreck."

"What's there to be nervous about?" I bent down to sip my drink and almost stabbed my eye-ball with the straw.

Jessica giggled. "Oh, sure, Callie. You would be nervous around that Garret guy."

"Invite him to your party," said Lindsay. "That would be real grown-up, Callie. All the girls going into seventh grade would think you really hung around with a cool crowd."

"Why? I don't even know him." I shook back my hair and tried to look casual. The truth was, someone as grown-up-looking as Garret would not even want to stand in my backyard, eating chips and dip and playing volleyball.

Lindsay rolled her eyes. "Callie, at least invite him. How many times do I have to explain things to you? You are turning thirteen, you are going to start junior high, it is soooooooo important that you start the seventh grade hanging around the coolest kids you can find. That way, you won't be left out."

I glanced over at Scott and Garret. Both of them would be considered cool by just about anyone. I looked at my reflection in the mirrored walls of the lobby. I would be considered ordinary by just about anyone. Maybe I did need their help.

I reached in my pocket for my Milk Duds. My party was getting more and more complicated. So was my life. Why did I have to surround myself with coolness? Did Lindsay actually think some of it would rub off on me?

Lindsay stabbed me with her pretzel. "Go over there, Callie dear, and ask Scott and Garret to come early and help you set up some horseshoes."

"I don't even own horseshoes, Lindsay," I groaned.

"You do now," she laughed. "That's what I'm getting you for your birthday."

"Oh, gee, thanks. Just what I never wanted."

"Okay, Callie, I'll make it a dart game then. Anything that requires Scott to set it up."

"Lindsay, I know you're trying to help me . . . grow up, I guess, but I really don't need any help."

"Yes, you do. I'm your coach, remember?" Lindsay gave me a push toward Scott. "You need my help so much you don't even realize you need it. Now hurry up before they leave."

Lindsay gave me another push, more like a shove, and I was propelled across the lobby.

I skidded to a stop in front of Scott. "Hey, hi there, Scott. Did you see a good movie?"

Scott glanced over at Garret and shrugged. "Well, we haven't decided on one yet."

Garret laughed. "Scott hasn't decided yet. I have. He isn't sure he'll understand it."

Scott shoved his hands into his pockets and stared at the floor. "Be quiet, Garret. I said I'd go."

"We just saw a funny one." I waited a second, getting ready to launch into a short, yet entertaining review. I would not bother telling them I had cried at the ending.

Garret snorted. "Yeah, well, the one we want to see isn't real funny. But very educational."

Just then another guy ran up to them, waving three tickets in the air. "Come on, guys, I got the tickets."

Scott looked suddenly worried, as if this kid had just waved a traffic ticket in his face.

"See ya," said Garret, turning from me and grabbing Scott.

Scott shot me a final, fed-up kind of look before he disappeared into the crowd.

I walked slowly across the lobby, joining Jessica and Lindsay.

"What happened?" Lindsay wanted to know right away.

"I'm not sure." It had been a very short conversation.

"Well, are they coming to your party or not?" Lindsay stood on tiptoe and stared over my shoulder. "Oh, my gosh!"

Jessica and I both turned around.

"What?" All I could see was a thousand kids.

"Scott and Cutie-pie just walked into theater three," whispered Lindsay. "Theater three!"

I turned back and started to walk to the exit. "Wow, Lindsay. Imagine people coming to a theater and actually going in to see a movie."

Lindsay and Jessica ran to catch up. "Yeah, but Callie, those guys went in to see an NC-17 movie. That awful movie that was made in France, with everyone trying to kill each other and no one wearing clothes. My mom said it was really bad."

I turned around, my eyes scanning the movie titles.

"Well, if you have to be seventeen, how did they get in?" asked Jessica. "Scott doesn't look seventeen."

I shrugged, remembering Garret's friend. The one who did look seventeen. He bought the tickets.

"Garret said the film was educational."

Lindsay and Jessica started to laugh.

"I'm *sure* that's why they went," giggled Lindsay.

"But it's in French. How can they understand it?" I asked. "I bet those movies don't even have a plot."

"Oh, Callie," sighed Lindsay. "Wake up, darling cousin. I don't think they care about the plot."

"Come on, let's get going," I said, shoving the door open. I wasn't Scott's baby-sitter. If he wanted to watch a dirty movie, let him.

"Lots of kids sneak into adult films," explained Jessica.

"I won't," I said.

Lindsay grinned. "Oh, yeah, well that's because you haven't turned thirteen yet. You don't know what you're going to do."

"Trust me, ladies," I said. "This is one girl who is going to stay the same, no matter what."

"We'll see," said Lindsay. "Turning thirteen always means you change a little."

"Says who?" I wanted to know.

"Everyone," Lindsay answered smugly. "You'll see."

"Oh, sure," I said. "I bet you a million dollars I don't change a bit."

The way things turned out, I'm lucky I never shook hands on that bet.

5

Once we hit the mall, we got busy, fast. We looked in five stores for my outfit before we decided to take a break and get a yogurt cone.

"I can't believe Scott snuck in to see that movie," I said.

"Are you going to tell his mom?" asked Jessica.

"No way," I said. "I'm not on bus patrol anymore." Holy cow, it was hard enough looking after my younger cousins, let alone trying to keep the rest of the population out of trouble. "Scott can go see whatever he wants. I don't care."

"Yes!" cheered Lindsay, slapping me on the back. "Now you're sounding like a real teenager! Watch out for Number One."

I glared at Lindsay. "Don't get any ideas, Lins. I would tell *your* mom if you snuck into one of those movies."

"Okay, okay. I get the message." Lindsay grabbed my cone and took a big bite. "Let's find your birthday outfit."

We walked through two more stores before we finally found something that looked nice on me. Being too tall and too skinny is not the best combination for easy shopping.

"Ohhhh, Callie, look at that!" Lindsay was pointing to a short denim skirt with a navy-and-white tank top. "You would look great in that with your red hair."

"What? Are you kidding?" I asked. "Red, white, and blue. I would look like the American flag!"

Jessica giggled. "Try it on. Patriotism is in."

I had to admit, once I tried on the outfit, I looked pretty cute. Even the salesgirl asked if I modeled. Lindsay laughed so hard, she hung onto the dressing room curtain and pulled it off the rod. The salesgirl spent ten minutes trying to reattach it and then went to help someone else.

"Gosh, I couldn't help it," Lindsay said, trying to slow her haw-hawing down to a giggle. "I can't picture you modeling, Callie. I mean, you would fall off a runway and kill yourself."

I frowned. "Unless I tried to kill someone else. Like a little cousin with a big mouth."

Lindsay laughed even harder.

"But that was real nice she thought you were pretty enough," added Jessica. "You are, Callie. And you are so lucky to be tall!"

I smiled at my reflection in the mirror. I did look older. Maybe people would think I looked thirteen.

After we paid for the outfit, we walked around the upper level of the mall. I hugged my shopping bag to my chest and smiled. Tomorrow was going to be a great day. "I hope it doesn't rain for the party. It will be more fun if we can go outside."

"Guaranteed fun if you invite Garret Novak," promised Lindsay. "I could see the blue of his eyes from across the lobby."

"You could not!"

"He really is cute," said Jessica. "You should ask him, Callie. Since he's new in town."

"I'll call him for you," offered Lindsay. "I'll pretend to be you and say that I really enjoyed meeting him in the lobby of Cinema World." Lindsay pretended she had a phone to her ear. "Oh, Garret, hi there. This is Callie, that lovely redhead you met right before you went in to see that dirty movie. Yes, well, I noticed how terribly handsome you were and I was just wondering if you would please come to my party, and then, well, if you're not busy for the rest of your life, well . . . maybe MARRY me."

Jessica started to laugh.

I grabbed Lindsay and hung up her pretend phone. "I didn't meet him," I corrected. "Garret doesn't know I exist."

"He's here!" squeaked Jessica, stopping dead in her tracks. "In person."

"Who's where?" I asked.

Jessica pointed toward the escalator. Slowly

rising from the second floor came Scott, Garret, and the tall kid.

"I wonder what happened?" whispered Lindsay. "The movie can't be over this fast."

"They look mad about something," I pointed out.

"Maybe they got kicked out," said Jessie. "Maybe the usher asked for I.D."

"I don't know," I said. "Let's ask them."

"What?" cried Lindsay. "You're kidding."

At first, I was kidding, but seeing how shocked Lindsay was, I decided to go with it. At the time, it seemed a very brave and thirteen-year-old thing to do.

"Wait a minute, Callie!" Lindsay yanked me backwards. "You can't march over there and ask them why they aren't still watching the dirty movie."

"Why not?"

"She's right," added Jessica. "You can't ask."

"Why?" I asked again.

"Because MaryBeth said it's rude to ask questions like that to boys. You have to be more subtle. It shows you're grown-up."

"Subtle?" I knew Lindsay couldn't spell it, let alone tell me what it meant.

"Yeah," said Lindsay. "You have to relax, chill out, stay cool. . . ."

"What are you, Lins," I sputtered, "some sort of walking T-shirt? Why are you always telling me what to do lately? You're not an expert on being a teenager, you know."

"I'm your coach," sputtered Lindsay. "Remember?"

"Well, go coach yourself in how to mind your own business," I snapped back.

Somebody yanked my ponytail hard.

"Hey, security sent us over!" laughed Scott. "I could hear you yelling all over the mall, Callie. No fights allowed."

"What?" I lowered my fist and tried to smile.

"We come in peace!" Garret held up both hands and started laughing.

"Looks like your temper matches your hair," teased the oldest kid, Mr. Ticket-Getter.

"She's harmless," joked Scott. "The vet makes sure Callie gets all her shots."

"Ha ha," I said. "I see the vet finally removed your muzzle, Scott."

We all laughed then.

"Must have been a very short movie, Scott," I joked.

His face flushed red. "Yeah, sort of. I spotted my aunt and uncle two rows in front of us. I thought I'd better get out of there."

"Smart move," agreed Lindsay.

Since Scott didn't bother to introduce us, I did. "Hi, I'm Callie, and this is Jessica and Lins."

"Oh, sorry." Scott grinned and shook his head. "This is Garret Novak and his brother, Larry.

They've just moved here from Richmond, Virginia."

"Hi," we all said at once.

"Like it so far?" I asked.

"Sure," said Garret. "I don't know too many kids, yet."

"Come to Callie's party tomorrow," cried Lindsay.

Scott laughed. "Yeah, the Red Baron turns thirteen."

"That would be great if you could come over." I ripped a corner off my bag. "Do you have a pen? I'll write my number down."

"Who's screaming?" asked Jessica, turning around.

"Holy cow, look at that guy," cried Scott. "Someone must be after him."

"Oh, my gosh," Lindsay said, grabbing onto Jessica. "Let's get out of here."

But before anyone could move, a huge teenager wearing a hooded sweatshirt came charging straight for us.

"Watch out!" screamed Garret, lunging into me. We both slammed down hard on the floor, toppling a metal trash can.

"Whoa, did you get the license plate of that kid?" groaned Garret, sitting up and rubbing his shoulder. He turned and offered me his hand. "You okay?"

I tried to sit up, but my hand was killing me.

Lindsay ran over and tried to pull me up by the arm.

"Don't, don't," I said softly. Red hot wires of pain were shooting up my left arm.

"What a jerk that guy was," said Scott. "He didn't even stop to see if you were all right."

"Can you get up, Callie?" Jessica asked.

I closed my eyes, embarrassed by the stinging tears.

"Here, you can't stay on the floor," said Garret. "Somebody else is going to step on you."

Garret and Scott bent down and lifted me up by the waist.

"My arm really hurts," I said again. "Jessica, maybe you and Lins better go and find Aunt Shelly."

"I'm not going to leave you," insisted Lindsay.

"She'll be okay," said Garret. "We'll stay with her, over there by the bench."

"Okay," said Lindsay. She brushed back my tussled hair and smiled. "We'll be right back, Callie."

I nodded, then started walking slowly with Garret, cradling my left arm. My wrist was killing me.

"I'll go get you a Coke," offered Scott. He was chewing on his lower lip and looking pretty worried.

"Get me one, too," said Garret.

"I'll come and help," said Larry.

I slid down on the bench and Garret sat down next to me.

"Must hurt, huh?" Garret bent down and looked at my arm. "Sorry. I guess I fell on you."

"You were only trying to . . ." I almost said, "save me," but that sounded too dramatic.

Garret sighed and leaned back against the bench. "You'll be okay."

"Yeah." I glanced up at him and smiled. MaryBeth was right. He was the cutest boy I had ever talked to.

Garret sat up. "What's wrong?" He rubbed his hand over his face. "Do I have popcorn stuck on my face or something?"

I started to laugh. "No. You look okay."

Garret gave me a lopsided grin. "Thanks. I wish your arm looked a little better. I'm real sorry."

"That's okay." I looked up at him, then back down at the floor. I had heard about love at first sight. But they were safe sightings, in corny old movies and library books.

Yet, the way my heart was pounding and traveling so fast up my throat, I was afraid it was happening to me.

6

Aunt Shelly was worried something was broken, so she got security to bring a wheelchair. I felt like a real idiot being wheeled through the mall in it. But my arm really hurt and everyone was being so nice to me, I knew they wouldn't tease me about it later.

"Does this mean your party is cancelled?" asked Scott.

"Of course not," said Lindsay. "Make sure all three of you come, okay? Seven o'clock."

"I have to work," said Larry.

"I'll be there," promised Scott.

"I'll come," said Garret. He smiled at me as if he was really excited about it. "I'll be your bodyguard."

Larry started to laugh and slapped Garret on the back. "Yeah, my little brother is a regular knight in shining armor, all right."

Garret handed me my bag. "Here you go."

"See you boys later," called out Aunt Shelly. "Girls, hold the doors."

"I will," said Garret. He pulled back the wide glass doors and grinned at me as I was wheeled past.

"See you tomorrow, birthday girl," he said.

"Callie will be thirteen!" added Jessica. "Sweet thirteen and never been kis — "

"See you tomorrow!" I shouted out.

"Thanks," said Garret. He smiled at me then, and I suddenly felt as if I were in one of those commercials where clouds are blowing all around you and music is playing. But the only thing I was aware of was Garret Novak's blue eyes.

It took a long time to get me in the front seat, buckled up, and the wheelchair taken back. I just sat there, holding my aching arm, and smiling.

"What's wrong, Callie?" Lindsay asked as we headed down the long drive to the highway. "You aren't going into shock, are you?"

Jessica started to giggle.

"What?" asked Aunt Shelly, reaching her hand out to feel my forehead.

"I'm okay," I said softly. "Garret was so nice to me."

Lindsay gave a short laugh. "The kid *fell* on you and probably broke your arm. How nice was that?"

"He was trying to save me," I added.

Jessica leaned forward from the backseat and put her hand on my shoulder. "He was really brave. Scott didn't try to get anyone out of the way but himself."

"Oh, brother," muttered Lindsay. "No one tried to save me, either."

"I called your mother, Callie," Aunt Shelly said. "She is meeting us at the hospital."

"Great," I said.

"*Great?* Hey, wait a minute," said Lindsay. She poked her head between the two bucket seats and stuck her face into mine. "Wait a little minute, here."

"What are you looking at, Lindsay?" I asked, smiling from ear to ear.

Aunt Shelly reached over and patted my knee. "What's wrong?"

"I'll tell you what's wrong," Lindsay announced as she stuck her face right into mine and started laughing. "Our own Callie Gaitlin is in love!"

7

My parents were waiting for us at the hospital, so Aunt Shelly took Jessica and Lindsay home.

"Be brave, Callie!" Lindsay shouted out the window as the car pulled away.

It seemed to take forever to fill out the forms and get X-rayed. After at least two hours of waiting, the doctor told us I had chipped a bone in my wrist and needed a cast. It was the first time in my life I had ever broken anything, so it was pretty interesting. Of course, not nearly as interesting as being saved by someone as cute as Garret Novak.

I got to bed so late on Friday night, and had such a hard time sleeping with my new cast, I really slept in on Saturday.

"Good morning, birthday girl!" my father sang out as he carried in a breakfast tray.

"Happy birthday, honey," my mother said, leaning down and giving me a careful hug. "Too bad your first present was a broken wrist."

"It doesn't hurt so much now," I said, lifting up the cast. "This cast feels so heavy."

"Thirteen at last!" laughed my mother. "Jessica and Lindsay are downstairs already. They wanted to make sure you were feeling well enough for your party tonight."

"Of course," I said quickly. In fact, I could hardly wait for the party to start. I never did get a chance to give Garret my phone number. Maybe Scott would bring him.

"Hey, hey, hey," called Lindsay from the hall. "Mind if I take a peek at the birthday girl?"

Lindsay came in first, dropping an armload of movie magazines and videotapes on the end of my bed. "Be careful with these, cuz. They happen to be some of my favorites."

"Happy birthday, Callie! " Jessica said as she came into the room. "Here are some muffins my mom made for you."

"Thanks, guys," I said, reaching for a muffin. "But, I'm not sick. I just chipped a bone."

Lindsay raised an eyebrow. "Just chipped a bone. What a brave girl we have here."

"So the party's still on?" asked Jessica.

"Sure. I feel great." I did. Thirteen at last!

"Get dressed, Callie, and go sit in the sun," suggested my mother. "I want you to take it easy today."

"I'll make sure of that," said Lindsay. "This girl

needs to save all her strength for her party tonight."

Jessica and Lindsay acted like my ladies-in-waiting. They made my bed while I got dressed, and they even tied my tennis shoes.

Once we were outside, Lindsay stopped acting like a helpful cousin and turned back into my relentless coach.

"So, did Garret or Scott call last night to see if you were okay?" asked Lindsay. She pulled her notebook from her pocket and uncapped her pen.

"No." I could tell Lindsay was disappointed. "It was pretty late when we got home, so maybe they tried to call, but we weren't home or something."

"Maybe," said Lindsay. She scribbled a few lines. "I'm going to mark down that you were unavailable to receive calls."

"I hope they come tonight," said Jessica.

"They have to come," insisted Lindsay. "Look at Callie, here. I may have to wear earmuffs to the party tonight, her heart is beating so hard at the mere mention of Garret's name. The girl is in love, Jessie."

Jessica and I started to laugh. "I am *not* in love," I said slowly. "He's just a nice guy."

"Yeah, yeah," Lindsay said. "The world is filled with nice guys, Callie. But you have never worn this dreamy, sappy look on your face."

"I am *not* in love," I insisted.

"You're in love, all right. Besides, I already put

it in my notebook." Lindsay snapped her notebook closed. "But after thinking about it all night, I think maybe it might be a smart move, after all."

"A smart move?" I asked.

"Yeah, as your coach, I think it might be helpful and very grown-up if you had a crush on Garret. It will help you break in with the popular crowd once school starts. He broke your wrist, so he'll feel guilty enough to offer to carry your books in the hall, and maybe get your cafeteria tray for you."

"You're sooooooo lucky," said Jessica. "I bet if anyone ever broke my wrist, it would be someone awful."

"Yeah," sighed Lindsay. "Remember in the second grade when that smelly Jimmy Hansen stabbed me with his sharpened pencil and I thought I'd die from lead poisoning? There was absolutely no romance to that injury."

"Well, maybe some cute guy will break your leg one day," I joked. I shook my head, then peered down the street to see if anyone was coming up the lane.

"Oh, sit back, Callie. Garret-the-Gorgeous is not in the neighborhood," Jessica announced. "We checked behind every tree."

"Ha-ha," I said. But I did stretch out again. I wanted my cheeks to get pink so no one could tell when I was blushing tonight. What if Garret had heard Lindsay last night at the mall and he wanted to give me a birthday kiss? A first kiss was always special, but when someone as cute as Garret gave it, it would make time stand still. "Happy birthday, Callie," he would say, then lean forward, close his eyes and . . .

"Look, Jessie, she's smiling," snorted Lindsay. "She's dreaming of Garret and his dramatic rescue at the Sweetwater Mall."

"It was dramatic," I said, anxious to talk about it all over again. "I mean, Garret just dove for me as soon as he saw that crazy guy heading for me. That man could have broken my neck at the rate he was traveling!"

"Oh, brother," sighed Lindsay. "Don't exaggerate toooooo much, lady. The guy was probably just running out to put some more money in his parking meter."

"I am not exaggerating, Lins, and you know it," I said, reaching out to swat her with my good hand. "There are no meters at the mall. Garret was worried about me, that's all. He just did what he had to do to protect me."

"You just happened to be standing closest to him," said Lindsay. "I don't want to burst your bubble, dar-link, but if I had been standing next to him, I would have been the one he pushed out of the way. Not that I'm jealous, or anything."

"What?" I sat up straighter. "Lins, that isn't one bit true. Besides, I thought you wanted me to have a crush on Garret."

"I do, Callie." Lindsay flipped through her notebook. "I just think we have to keep the facts straight. Having a crush on Garret will work out great for your fresh start, your switch over into teenagerism, but you've got to face the facts, Callie."

"What facts?" In spite of the eighty-five-degree weather, my voice was very cool.

Lindsay picked up her iced tea and took a long drink. "Well, that Garret may not be ready to have a crush on you, or anyone yet. I mean, he is new in town. So, we might have to work a little to get him to like you as a girlfriend."

"He already likes me," I sputtered. "He saved me, Lins. How much more does he have to do?"

Lindsay rolled her eyes at Jessica. "Whatever. Okay, okay, so he saved you from some guy who was probably running to catch a bus, and . . ."

"That guy could have had a gun," I added. "Aunt Shelly said that crazy people like that could do anything."

Lindsay waved me away. "My mom was at the other end of the mall. I was there. I saw the whole thing."

"Jessie." I spun around and grabbed her arm. "You saw it, too. Wasn't Garret trying to save me?"

Jessica nodded. "Sure."

"Oh, pleasssssse," laughed Lindsay, closing her notebook. "I can't believe we are fighting over this. I mean, we are on the same team, Callie. I am your coach, dar-link."

I leaned back and drew in a deep breath. I kept my mouth closed tightly so I wouldn't just fire Lindsay on the spot. Why was she trying to ruin my crush, anyway? It was my birthday, for pete's sake!

"Okay, let's plan the party games," Lindsay said brightly.

"Volleyball," said Jessica. "And basketball."

"Good." Lindsay nodded. "Callie, maybe we should pick out some slow dances so Garret can ask you to dance. Wait a minute. That might be too risky. Yeah, you better not take a chance. Ask him before MaryBeth can grab him."

"He is not some door prize, Lins," I pointed out. "Garret can dance with anyone he wants."

Lindsay tapped her pencil on the metal arm of my chair. "Hey, you do not want to compete with MaryBeth. Believe me. Now, be sure and ask him, okay? I am trying to help you, Callie."

"Maybe we should wait and just make up things to do at the party once it starts," suggested Jessica.

"Girls, we can not leave anything to chance," warned Lindsay. "This whole evening has to be planned, right down to the last salted nut."

"Thanks a lot, Lins. I never knew I needed that much help." I tried to cross my arms and whacked my wrist. "Oh, see what you made me do!"

"I didn't do anything!" snapped Lindsay. "You are living in la-la land and I am trying to help you be cool."

"I am cool enough right now," I sputtered. My head ached. I wished Lindsay would just leave me alone so I could enjoy my birthday. "Just stop interfering, okay?"

Lindsay stood up and made a dramatic production of shoving her notebook and pencil deep into the pocket of her shorts. "Okay, I think that this meeting has ended. Call me later, Callie, when you're ready to accept my help."

"Don't hold your breath," I muttered. "You're such a drill sergeant!"

"You are being so ungrateful," Lindsay snapped. "You think it's easy to switch you from being ordinary Callie to the new, improved, deluxe Callie?"

"I am not ordinary!" My voice must have been pretty loud because the neighbor's dog started barking.

"Don't fight," said Jessica. Ever since her parents got divorced, she hated to hear anyone argue.

"Talk to Lindsay, Jessie," I said calmly. I even smiled at her since she was being the nicest. "It's just a little annoying that Lins is jealous of me."

Lindsay made a high squeaking noise and then started to flounce across the yard. "Ha! You're crazzzzzzy, girl. That's it, I'm leaving."

I leaned forward and whispered close to Jessica's ear. "She just wishes someone as handsome as Garret Novak saved her life."

"I heard that!" shouted Lindsay from the hedge. She put her hands on her hips and glared down at me. "If I didn't know you were in love and *totally* not thinking straight, I'd be mad at you. The truth is, Callie, that Garret paid just as much attention to me as he did to you. While my mom was getting you in the wheelchair, Garret asked me all about myself. He even asked if I wanted the rest of his Coke."

"He did not!" I had heard Garret crunching his ice way before Aunt Shelly got the wheelchair. His Coke cup was empty. "He probably just asked you to throw it away for him."

"Same difference," snapped Lindsay.

I groaned. "You are so weird, Lins. It's not the same thing at all." I could feel my temper straining to get out.

"Stop fighting," pleaded Jessica. She got up and looked around the yard. "Let's go do something fun."

"Yeah, let's get ready for my party," I said quickly. "Jessie, will you stay and help? I would love for someone normal to help me get ready."

"I am ten times more normal than you, Callie!" Lindsay reached into her pocket and threw the notebook on the grass. "In fact, I'm so normal that I can't possibly coach you into trying to be cool. So, don't worry about me sticking around. I have better things to do."

"So do I!" I called back. "You're fired!"

Lindsay threw her leg over her bike and shook back her long blonde hair. "I quit! You have to go make up a whole bunch of romantic lies, Callie. Wake up, cuz. If you weren't so blinded by love, you would know that Garret likes us both the same."

I slowly stood up, holding my wrist and trying to look as grown-up as possible. "Lins, Garret probably doesn't even remember your name. He thinks you're Leslie, or Lee-Lee!"

"Yeah?" shot back Lindsay. "Well, the real reason Garret didn't call you last night is because he forgot your name, too. He thinks your name is . . . is Catus, or Cal-a-mine lotion."

"In your dreams!" I yelled. I bit my lip, trying to remember if Garret did call me anything.

"Girls!" Jessica stood up, too. "You guys are just teasing, aren't you?"

"No!" I snapped, letting my temper take over. "I'm sick of a puny twelve-year-old telling me what to do."

I knew I should have stopped talking as soon as I saw how hurt Lindsay looked. Why was I being so mean? I should have laughed and said, "Hey, you know I'm kidding, Lins." Maybe then the whole thing would have blown over. But I didn't. My temper reacts ten times faster than my brain.

I stood there and watched her ride her bike right over the tiny pink notebook that contained my future.

"Happy birthday if I never see you again!" Lindsay shouted across the yard.

"Thanks for nothing!" I called back.

I sank back in my chair and tried not to look upset. But I was. From that moment on, I was flying high without a net, trying to be thirteen without a coach.

8

Hours later, I didn't know which hurt most, my wrist, my sunburn, or remembering how mean I had been to Lindsay. The whole stupid fight was my fault. I shouldn't have fired her. She was only trying to help me. Why couldn't I have said, "Okay, Lins, we can both like Garret. I mean, the guy is cute enough to share." Why did I have to have such a temper? Where was the wire leading from my big mouth to my brain?

I picked up the phone to call Lindsay twelve times before my party started; I hung up twelve times. Every time I thought about apologizing, I would remember the mean things she had said to me. The truth was, Lindsay had insulted me. She couldn't let it go, she couldn't say, "Whoa, Callie, congratulations on getting someone as hot as Garret to like you. I'm proud to have a cousin like you."

And the sad truth was, after replaying the rescue scene in my head forty-seven times, I was pretty sure that Garret had acted out of natural instinct. Lindsay was right. I wasn't anything special to him. I bet if a ninety-two-year-old lady wearing knee highs, smelling of Vicks VapoRub, had been standing next to Garret when the guy in the blue sweatshirt raced by, he would have shoved her out of the way, too.

But the old lady would have been smart enough to give Garret a dollar, or make him a dozen cupcakes to say thank you. Not fall in love with him.

"You are soooo stupid, Callie," I muttered to myself. I put a cold washcloth on my face and sighed. Gosh, when would I know the right way to act? If I were smart, I'd call Lindsay right now and let her be the first to know that I wasn't even crazy about Garret anymore. I barely knew him. I missed Lindsay and I couldn't imagine having a party without her. When would I learn to control my temper?

I glanced at the clock. Six-fifteen. I brushed my hair back with my right hand and added a quick dab of lip gloss.

I ran into my parents' room and dialed Lindsay's number. This time I didn't hang up. I let it ring ten times, but nobody answered.

"Maybe she's on her way over," I said as I hung up. Lindsay usually liked to be the first to come, the last to leave any party.

I raced downstairs to help my mom set out the food. My mom doesn't like to cook, but she is the master of snack food. She can take a green pepper from the garden, stuff it full of onion dip, and still find time to carve an apple into a little bird. The patio looked wonderful: tables filled with cheese and grapes, popcorn, and cold vegetable pizza.

"Boy, have you been busy, Mom. Thanks, it looks so nice."

My mom gave me my twenty-fourth hug. "You're welcome, Callie. I hope your night is special, honey. Turning thirteen is a very special day."

"I know; I'm excited." I smiled back, tempted to tell her about my awful fight with Lindsay. But I didn't. My mother would say, "You lost your temper again? You are the oldest cousin, Callie. It's up to you to set the right example!"

"Hey, Callie," called my dad from the driveway. "Jessica's here!"

My dad had spent the last hour watering the entire yard to cool things down. It was almost six-thirty and still eighty degrees.

"Thanks, Dad."

"Happy birthday, Callie!" Jessie handed me a small box and gave me a quick hug. "Pretend you don't know earrings are inside."

"What a surprise," I joked. Jessica, Lindsay, and I had given each other earrings every year since we got ours pierced.

I opened the box and held up the tiny white cat

earrings. "They look just like Lindsay's weird cat." I glanced down the driveway. "Is Lins coming?"

Jessica shrugged. "I think she's pretty mad about you yelling at her."

"She yelled at me, too!"

"I know, but . . . " Jessica glanced around. "Things look great."

"Thanks," I said softly. I couldn't believe Lindsay was actually going to miss one of my birthday parties. Even when she was five and had the chicken pox, she snuck out and rode her bike over to my house.

How could I possibly turn thirteen without Lindsay?

"Call her, Callie," urged Jessica. "Please. I know she would forgive you right away."

"Okay." Jessica was right. I couldn't believe I had yelled at Lindsay over something as stupid as a boy. Even a handsome, brave, and incredibly blue-eyed boy like Garret Novak.

"Hey, this must be the place!" Brad and Michael raced past me, dribbling a basketball. "Happy birthday, Gaitlin."

"Hi!" Before I could even walk to the kitchen, more and more kids started walking up the driveway. The party had begun.

Scott walked around the side yard with Garret. He was holding a three-foot paper bird at the end of a wire. I wasn't quite sure if it was my birthday present or if it had just followed the boys to the party.

"Whoa, a cast and everything! Look at you," hooted Scott. He handed me the paper bird. "This is for you," Scott said. He shook his head. "I can't believe my mom bought this stupid thing. It's filled with candy and you're supposed to whack it apart."

"How did you know I've wanted one for years?" I joked.

"It's called a *piñata*," said Jessica. "I had a Santa Claus one last year. They're fun, Scott."

Garret lifted up my cast. "Hey, you really did get hurt. I'm sorry about your wrist, Callie."

"Let me hang the bird before Garret trips over it and breaks your other wrist, Callie," offered Scott. He walked around the yard and finally settled on the low limb of an ash tree.

"Happy birthday!"

We all turned and watched as MaryBeth and Luisa raced up the driveway. MaryBeth was wearing a pale yellow tank dress that made her tan look even darker.

"Whoa," muttered Garret. He was looking straight at MaryBeth.

Automatically, I glanced down at my own tank top and denim skirt. It would be so much fun to walk around looking like MaryBeth for a day.

"Happy birthday, Callie," said MaryBeth. She

handed me a large pink box, wrapped in the hot-pink paper from Rosebud's, one of Sweetwater's nicest shops. "Oh, my gosh, what happened to your wrist?"

"Some guy tried to knock her over," hooted Scott. "A hit-and-run in the mall."

"Garret saved her," added Jessica.

MaryBeth's eyebrows shot up. "He did?"

"Hey, that reminds me," said Garret. He reached into the pocket of his plaid shorts and handed me a small gold package. "Happy birthday."

As if the present were magnetized, every girl within earshot drew around me.

"Why, isn't that sweet?" said MaryBeth, flashing Garret a smile. "First you save Callie's life, and then you bring her a present."

I looked up, waiting for Garret to melt in front of MaryBeth's million-dollar smile. But Garret was looking at me.

"Aren't you going to open it?" he asked. "I got it last night."

I tore off part of the paper. "It's kind of hard to do with only one hand," I said nervously.

"I'll help," said Garret quickly. "I couldn't find the box it came in, so I just put it in my dad's watch box."

"How clever," giggled MaryBeth.

"He's clever all right," agreed Scott.

Garret opened the black BULOVA box, and

lifted a thin gold bracelet from the black velvet.

"Oh, it's beautiful!" I cried. Actually, Mary-Beth, Luisa, Jessica, and about five other girls all said it with me at the same time. It was like the Sweetwater Choir.

"Do you like it?" asked Garret. "Here, let me put it on your wrist."

I held up both arms and smiled. "Take your pick."

Garret grinned and fastened the bracelet to my right wrist.

"Thanks, Garret," I managed to say. My face was so hot, I knew my cheeks had to be bright red.

"Hey, how about some hoop action?" Brad called out. "Five to a team."

Garret handed me the black box and shot across the yard.

"Lucky you, Callie. That's some present," MaryBeth said approvingly. "I didn't even realize you knew him."

"I met him last night," I said. I lifted my arm and watched as the thin bracelet swayed back and forth on my wrist.

"Gosh," Luisa sighed. "Garret is sooooo cute."

MaryBeth nodded. "He sure is." She tapped her own pink box. "I'm afraid my present isn't nearly as exciting."

I laughed, and then glanced down at my bracelet. Nothing could be more exciting than my gift from Garret.

"So, ladies, what did I miss?"

"Lins!" I cried. I raced across the yard and gave her a big hug.

"Sorry," I laughed. "Me and my big mouth."

"Yeah, I know," Lindsay said. Then she grinned and hugged me back. "I'm sorry, too."

"Come on, I have so much to tell you," I gasped. I held up my wrist. "Garret gave me this!"

Lindsay's eyes widened. For a second, I was afraid our fight was about to go into round two. But then Lindsay hugged me again, even tighter. "That's great, Callie. The guy's got mar-ve-lous taste!"

"Will you please be my coach again, Lins?" I grabbed her arm. "If I promise to keep my temper and listen to every word you say?"

Lindsay frowned. "I don't know. We might get into another fight."

"Not this time," I promised. "Never again."

Lindsay stuck out her hand. "Shake on it!"

I stuck out my right hand, smiling and watching as my beautiful gold bracelet danced back and forth on my wrist.

Now that Lindsay and I were best friends again, my birthday party was absolutely perfect.

9

"I love being thirteen," I giggled. I dropped five more empty cans of soda in the trash can. "See how agile I am with only one hand?"

"You're incredible, lady," laughed Lindsay. "So far, it's been a great day for you. I mean, you're wearing a cool new outfit, the cutest boy in Sweetwater gave you a solid gold bracelet, and you happen to have two of the most di-vine cousins in the world right in front of your face."

Jessica dropped a handful of paper plates into the metal can. "This is a good party, Callie. The boys are being so much fun. Scott's *piñata* was a riot."

I glanced over at the basketball game in my driveway. Scott and Garret were the captains, blowing whistles and making up funny rules.

"MaryBeth has been following Garret like a shadow," muttered Lindsay. "Did you see when she pretended to twist her ankle, just so he would help her off the driveway?"

I shrugged, but I had seen the whole thing. So what? I didn't own Garret. Besides, he was always smiling at me.

"I don't see how she's playing in that dress," I said.

"She never would have worn that last year," said Lindsay.

"She didn't own it last year," I laughed.

Lindsay shook back her head. "Don't get me wrong, I like MaryBeth a lot. But I think she's getting conceited all of a sudden. Maybe it's because the lifeguards are always teasing her at the pool."

"She can't help it if she's beautiful," Jessica added fairly.

"I know, I know," muttered Lindsay. "But jeez . . .

I laughed and tugged Lindsay's hair. "Come on, let's put on some more tapes. Maybe someone will ask you for a dance."

Lindsay grinned. "Yeah, like Jessica here."

Once the music started playing, my mother brought out my cake. Of course, my dad had to be filming every second of the kids singing to me, and me blowing out the candles. Scott put one lit candle on my cast and Garret blew it out. I was glad my dad was filming that part. Garret's cheek brushed right against my hand.

"I hope your birthday wish comes true, honey," my dad said, giving me a big kiss.

"I think it already has," teased MaryBeth. She looked right at me, then glanced over at Garret and turned back to smile at me. That was nice of her, I thought. Kind of letting me know that she knew I liked Garret.

"Hey, wake up!"

Garret slid down on the picnic bench next to me. "Make sure you don't get frosting all over my present, Cal."

Cal! Garret already had a nickname for me. Nobody but my Grandma Lucy ever called me Cal.

"Should I take it off?" I lifted my wrist. A tiny glob of pink rose frosting was stuck to it already.

"Nah, you'll lose it." Garret reached over and grabbed my fork. "Here, I'll feed you."

"No!" I practically shouted it. The thought of Garret feeding me a bite of cake was too much. I was sure MaryBeth and Lindsay would classify that as totally unsubtle behavior.

Garret jumped back and stood up. "Okay, okay. I wasn't about to attack you with the fork, Cal."

I stood up, too, dropping my cake on the grass. Real cool. "I know that. It's just that, well, I'm not hungry anymore."

Garret scratched his head. "You're nuts."

"Of course she is," agreed Lindsay, who had just appeared out of nowhere. "She is just a fun, totally cool girl, I mean, teenager."

"Hey, Garret, get over here!" shouted a group

of guys from the driveway. "We need another player."

"Want to watch?" asked Garret.

"She can't," said Lindsay. She put her arm around me and patted it. "She has to go . . . go soak her wrist."

Garret raised one eyebrow. "Oh, okay."

I squirmed out from under Lindsay's arm as soon as Garret walked away. "I have to soak my wrist?"

Lindsay shrugged. "Hey, it's all I could come up with in a hurry. I needed to talk to you. Coach talk."

I groaned. "Lins, this is my party. I want to enjoy it."

Jessica came hurrying over, balancing three cans of grape soda and holding a bag of pretzel rods in her teeth.

"Sit down, Callie," ordered Lindsay. "Jessica and I want to have a little cuz huddle time."

"Oh, brother." I took a can of soda and tried not to laugh.

"Now." Lindsay popped open her own can of soda and started pacing back and forth. "I am not going to use the notebook approach any longer — "

"Good!" Jessica and I both shouted.

Lindsay frowned and shoved up her sleeves. "However, my eyes are like a well-trained camera."

"Is this going to take all night?" I joked.

"If you don't stay quiet, yes," said Lindsay. "Now, I have been studying the party so far and I've come up with a few conclusions."

"Only a few?" asked Jessica, smiling.

"First of all" — Lindsay scooted in between Jessica and me on the stone wall — "Garret does like you, Callie. I mean, at first, no offense, I thought he was just being nice to you since he tripped you at the mall."

"He was saving me," I inserted.

"Yeah, whatever," said Lindsay, snapping her pretzel in half. "But tonight, seeing that bracelet he gave you and how he keeps coming over to talk to you, I think he really does like you."

I smiled. "I hope so." I felt the fine gold chain of the bracelet.

"But" — Lindsay held her pretzel rod high in the air — "we've got to face facts."

"What facts?" asked Jessica. "Can't we all just have fun?"

"Fact number one is," Lindsay started to whisper, "that MaryBeth likes Garret, too. I heard her tell Luisa that she is sooooooo jealous of you, Callie."

"No!" Why would someone like MaryBeth be jealous of anyone?

"And," Lindsay tapped her pretzel on my cast, "I think that unless you are careful, he might like her back."

"Uh-oh," whispered Jessica. "We may be too late."

I swung my head around and tried to find Garret in the crowd. I found him too quickly. He was standing right under the garage door spotlight, eating a piece of *my* birthday cake and smiling down at MaryBeth.

10

An hour later, MaryBeth was ready to leave.

"Thanks, Callie, it was a great party," said MaryBeth. "I'll see you at the pool tomorrow."

"You're leaving?" I asked. "It's only ten o'clock."

MaryBeth giggled and pointed to Garret. "Ask Garret. He said he has to get home before the werewolves start to roam."

Garret was waving good-bye to Scott and Brad. I had been busy talking to a few kids since I cut the cake. I guess that was long enough for Garret to get a crush on MaryBeth instead of me.

"Oh, okay," I said after a second or two. How stupid could I get? Any boy would fall for MaryBeth. She was pretty, fun, and very nice.

"See ya," said MaryBeth. She ran over and stood next to Garret.

"Gosh, that was fast," muttered Jessica.

"It's okay," I lied. I looked down at my bracelet, wondering if I should still wear it. Maybe it was only meant for tonight. By tomorrow, MaryBeth would have lots of funny stories to tell about the walk home. Maybe Garret would buy her something special, too. He wouldn't even wait for her birthday. He might give it to her tomorrow. Just for being MaryBeth.

"Go say good-bye to him," insisted Lindsay. "Remind him that you're still here."

"Of course I'm still here, Lins," I snapped. "I live here."

"I know that," she said, giving me a push toward Garret. "But at least go over and say something."

"No." Why should I run around begging people to please stay at my party?

"Honestly," sighed Lindsay. "You aren't doing this right."

"Says who?" I sputtered. "And you don't know the right thing to do anyway."

"Stop it," said Jessica. "You two just made up."

I drew in a deep breath. "Sorry." I was, too. Lindsay was only trying to help me.

"Here he comes," whispered Lindsay. "Say something!"

"Thanks, Cal," said Garret. "I've got to get home."

"Okay," I said glumly. " 'Bye."

"It was a nice party," Garret said. "Thanks."

"You're welcome."

"See you later," he added.

I kept my eyes on the grass. "Have fun."

Garret started to leave, then he turned back. "Want me to help you clean up or anything? Since your wrist is in a cast."

"Garret," said MaryBeth. "What about the werewolves?"

"Want me to help?" Garret asked again.

"Sure," said Lindsay. "Callie needs lots of help."

I finally looked up. Garret was being real nice. Too bad he was being real nice to both me and MaryBeth. Maybe that's just the way boys acted in Richmond.

"You don't have to," I said at last. I picked up a paper plate and handed it to Jessica. "I have my assistants here."

Garret grinned. "Okay. See ya."

I stacked up a few paper plates and threw them in the trash. I didn't want to just stand there and watch MaryBeth walk away with Garret.

"You didn't even get your birthday kiss," Jessica said sadly. "Not even a handshake."

"Be quiet, Jessica," said Lindsay. "Callie doesn't have to like Garret. She can like anyone she wants to."

"I never did like him, anyway," I said slowly. "Not really."

Lindsay put her hand on my arm. "Not even a little?"

I smiled and shook back my hair. "No. I barely know him."

Jessica shook her head. "He sure is cute, though. And he gave you such a nice present. He has to like you some."

I ran my finger up and down the thin gold bracelet. It shimmered in the moonlight. "Yeah, well, maybe not."

"Who are you talking about?"

I jumped. Scott was standing in front of us, holding a Coke, and looking sweaty.

"No one," I said quickly.

"Yes, you were," he said. He drained the Coke can and crushed it. "Garret likes you, all right."

"He does?" I smiled at Scott. Scott must know Garret better than any of us.

"Sure," said Scott, tossing his can into the trash bin. "Likes you well enough to steal for you."

"What?"

I felt a chill shoot up my spine, zooming down each arm and racing right under the bracelet like a speeding freight train. "What are you saying, Scott?"

Scott scratched the back of his head and shrugged. "I'm saying that Garret stole the bracelet he gave you."

11

Lindsay and Jessica trailed me for the rest of the party, asking me ten thousand times when I was going to give Garret back the bracelet.

"Face it, Callie," Lindsay droned on. "You are always telling Jessica and me to do the right thing."

I sank down on the picnic bench, glad that the last guest had finally walked down the driveway. "Well, maybe accusing an innocent kid of a crime isn't the *right* thing to do, okay?"

"Ha!" Lindsay wiggled in beside me. "I think you should at least ask him about it, Callie."

"I'll handle it," I promised. "Now, thank you and good night."

I tossed and turned a lot that night. I'm not sure if it was my cast, or the fact that I wanted to believe that Garret liked me enough to spend real money on me.

I didn't want to believe Scott.

When I held my wrist up in the ray of moonlight

that filtered into my room, it looked so beautiful. It fit me just right.

But what if Scott was telling the truth? Are you supposed to write thank-you notes for stolen merchandise? *Dear Garret, Thanks for the bracelet. It fits me just fine. (Ha-ha, I guess that's a good thing since it's NOT returnable.)*

Staring out at the backyard the next morning brought the whole party back to me. How important I felt as Garret fastened the gold bracelet around my wrist.

"Does a guy steal presents if he thinks the girl isn't worth real money?" I wondered aloud. I had asked myself that question twenty times already in church.

"Callie?" My mother rapped on my door. "Did you say something?"

"No, Mom," I called back. "Just talking to myself."

"Okay, you're getting more like Grannie Gaitlin every day. Let me know if you need some company."

Before my mother could even walk down the hall, I yanked open the door. "Mom, can I talk to you now?"

My mother spun around so quickly, she dropped the top towel from the stack she was carrying. "Oh, sure, honey. Let me put these away and I'll be right there." She grinned at me. Moms love it when you actually track them down for a conversation.

"Are you okay?" she asked as she hurried into my room.

"Sure. Fine. I just wanted your opinion on something."

My mother sat on the end of my bed and folded her hands on her lap. "Our first teenage talk. What do you want to talk about, Callie?" My mother looked so pleased, as if I were ready to talk about something real personal, like hormones.

"Mom?" I sat down on the bed next to her. "Have you ever stolen anything?"

"What?" My mother popped up faster than toast. Then she took a deep breath, sat down, and rubbed her temples. "What?" she said more softly this time.

"I don't mean like a car or anything. But did you ever take, let's say, a candy bar from the dime store? Maybe a tube of lipstick from Thrift Drugs? How about a whole handful of mints when the sign says, ONLY ONE PLEASE!?"

"No." My mother was glancing around my room, probably wondering if I was hiding a leather jacket, or a neighbor's bike in my closet. "Why would you ask me something like that, Callie?"

"No reason," I waited a second. "Mom, do you think it's stealing if someone gives you too much change back and you just keep it?"

My mother's cheeks flushed a little pink on that one.

"Gosh, I honestly don't always count my change, Callie. I guess once or twice I may have ended up with a quarter extra." She turned and put her hand on my knee. "I don't understand what you're trying to say."

I shrugged, not sure myself. "I just wondered if someone as honest as yourself might have accidentally stolen something."

My mother bent her head, thinking hard.

"No," she said at last. "Unless I was real young and just forgot all about it."

"As young as me?"

My mother laughed. "Thirteen is certainly old enough to know right from wrong."

Oh, great! I was too old to pretend I was too young to know better. I wondered how old you had to be before you were supposed to investigate possible stealing.

"Mom, what would you do if a friend of yours stole something, and they told you. What would you do then?"

"Callie." My mother leaned closer, a slight smile beginning. "I wish you would just tell me what's bothering you, honey. Is a friend of yours stealing? I think I could help you if we talked more directly."

"Directly? I can directly tell you that I don't

know of anyone who steals." It was true. I didn't know for sure if Garret stole the bracelet, or if Scott was just joking around again, which was his favorite pastime. "I just wondered."

Frown lines appeared between my mother's eyes. "Your cousins aren't in trouble, are they?"

"No!" I laughed and leaned back against my bed, all relaxed, to let her know that things were just fine. My head was killing me, all tangled up with threads of things that weren't all tied up. Like, if I found out tomorrow that Garret really had stolen my bracelet, what would I do?

"I guess I haven't really been too much help, honey," said my mother with a slight, apologetic smile.

"Thanks, Mom," I said, hopping off my bed and heading for the door.

"Where are you going?"

"Over to Lins's. Jessica spent the night there last night. We're going to walk over to the pool for an hour."

"Great idea," said my mother. She stood up, too, turning and smoothing out the wrinkles from my bed. "Keep that cast dry, Callie. Just dip your feet in if you get too hot. Drink lots of fluids from the refreshment stand. Do you need money or can you just start running a tab?"

I laughed. That was a joke! Old Mr. Wisterman was a senior citizen who ran the refreshment stand and thought running a tab wasn't thrifty.

Don't buy what you can't pay for right then and there! was printed on an index card right beside the hot pretzel machine. I grinned, knowing Mr. Wisterman never turned a really thirsty kid away, ever. "Pay me back tomorrow," he would announce as he set down a soft drink in front of any little kid who had accidentally lost his money.

"Here, honey, take a dollar," my mother insisted.

"Thanks." I reached out for it.

"Callie!" Before I could snatch back my arm, my mother had grabbed my wrist. "Where did you get this?"

"This?" I said stupidly, knowing she meant the gold bracelet.

"It's so pretty. Was it a birthday present?"

"Yeah, it was," I said, as casually as I could muster.

"From whom?" my mother asked.

"Garret Novak. He's new in town. Didn't you meet him last night? He's real nice."

"The new boy from Richmond? I don't know if he should be giving you something so expensive, honey."

"Well, he's also the kid who pushed me out of the way at the mall," I pointed out. "So, maybe he felt guilty about me breaking my wrist."

Finally my mother smiled. "Maybe so. It was thoughtful of him, but a little extravagant."

I nodded, biting the inside of my lip so I

wouldn't add, "Don't worry, Scott said he stole it."

"Mom, maybe I shouldn't wear it. Since it's real gold." I would try to talk to Scott at the pool and find out if he had been kidding or not.

"Wear it. Enjoy it. Don't worry, you won't lose it. You're a big girl now, Callie." My mother smiled, then gave me a hug. "I remember when I was fourteen, a boy named Gary gave me a silver bracelet. I felt so grown-up."

As the clock started to chime, my mother stretched. "Gosh, it's getting late. Have fun at the pool, Callie. Don't get your cast wet."

"I won't." I grabbed my towel. "See you later."

I ran most of the way to Lindsay's house. Jessica and Lindsay were waiting for me on the wide front porch.

"I can't believe you're still wearing the bracelet!" declared Lindsay before I even made it up the front steps.

"Jeeeweeez, I told you, Jessica. I told you she would be wearing it."

"This?" I asked innocently, holding up my wrist.

"Yes, that!" Lindsay met me on the middle step and grabbed my wrist. "How can you wear stolen property?"

I pulled my wrist back. "I didn't steal it!"

"But it's stolen," repeated Lindsay. "Scott said."

"We don't know that for sure!"

"Why would Scott make it up?" asked Lindsay, hands on hips. "We know Scott a whole lot better than we know Garret."

"Garret is nice, Lins."

Lindsay laughed a short ha! "You mean, Garret is cute."

I glared at her, my temper causing the back of my neck to itch like a tick bite. "I mean, he's nice. He saved me, didn't he?"

"He broke your wrist, Callie. What do we know about this kid except he has royal-blue eyes?"

I passed her and tossed my towel down on the porch swing. "Here we go again. What is this, the police department?"

Jessica came and sat down next to me. "Callie, we just don't want you to get in trouble."

"Trouble? Who's getting in trouble? I didn't steal it. And it's just a rumor that Garret stole it. Is it tooooooo terribly impossible to believe that a boy would actually go out and spend money on me?" I gave the swing a push. "Jeez, you guys are making such a big deal out of this."

"Callie," said Lindsay. She hopped up on the railing and lowered her voice. "You have to ask Garret about it. Otherwise, how could you possibly keep it?"

I shrugged. "Garret gave it to me. You gave me a pair of earrings, did I ask you for a receipt?"

Lindsay groaned. "Oh, brother. I'm your cousin."

Jessica looked nervous. "Maybe Garret didn't mean to steal it."

"Scott was joking," I sputtered. "Or maybe he does like MaryBeth and made the whole thing up because MaryBeth left the party with Garret." I let my voice trail off. Even I didn't believe what I'd just said. Scott liked every girl the same.

"Come on, let's drop it. I want to go to the pool," said Jessica. "Besides, Callie doesn't have to decide today what she's going to do." Jessica smiled at me. "You'll do the right thing."

"I hope," declared Lindsay. "I'd throw the bracelet right back in Garret's face. I think it's really rude of him to give you something that's been stolen."

"We don't know that!" I said angrily. "Besides, you can't tell me that you would throw this in his face."

Lindsay hopped off the railing and raised her right hand. "Right hand to God, I would, Callie."

"Ha!" I stood up so fast the porch swing banged against the wall. "You would treasure anything Garret Novak gave you!"

"And before you turned into a hot-shot teenager, you would have thrown it even harder," said Lindsay. She pushed back her hair and shoved out her chin. "You know it, too."

"Stop it," said Jessica. "Come on, let's go."

"I would throw the bracelet in Garret's face and then walk away," Lindsay said smugly.

"Oh, aren't you the saint," I muttered as I headed down the stairs. "Come on, let's go."

"The sun is really hot," Jessica said cheerfully. "I bet the pool will be crowded."

"Did you wear your bracelet to church this morning, Callie?" Lindsay asked. Her voice sounded exactly like our Sunday school teacher's. The teacher no one liked because she was so mean.

"Yes." Boy, Lindsay was worse than a burr on your sock. Constant prickling. She was my coach, not my conscience!

"Well, then," Lindsay said with a smile. "I guess that proves something."

I glared at her. "It proves I was in a hurry to get to church," I lied. We were always one of the first families at church so my dad could sit by the fan.

Lindsay nudged Jessica. She practically knocked her off the sidewalk, she wanted me to see it so badly.

"I wouldn't wear something stolen, no matter how cute the thief was." Lindsay made a big production of refolding her towel.

"Jessica, are you signing up for camp the last two weeks of August?" I asked loudly.

"I think so," said Jessica slowly. "Are you two going?"

"I am," I said.

"I am, too," said Lindsay icily.

We stood at the crest of the hill, looking down

at the community pool. It was packed.

"I hope we find our spot near the shade," I said. "My mom said my cast might get real hot if I stay in the sun too long."

"Your bracelet is hot already," said Lindsay.

"Ha-ha," I said dryly.

But as we headed down the hill, I switched my towel over my right wrist and covered up the bracelet.

12

"It's so crowded today," I said, squinting my eyes against the glaring sun. "Where do you want to sit?"

"By the trees, of course," said Lindsay. She always liked the spot by the pine trees near the fence. It was our spot.

"Callie!"

MaryBeth stood up and waved us over.

"Come on, let's sit with her!" I suggested.

"She sits in the middle of the whole yard!" complained Lindsay. "It's a hundred degrees hotter there."

"It will be fun for a change," Jessica said quickly.

We headed over to MaryBeth and Luisa. "Don't tell MaryBeth what Scott said about the bracelet," I hissed as we headed over.

"Why not?" Lindsay looked anxious to tell her every tiny detail.

"Because it's none of her business," I said

calmly. "We don't even know if it's the truth. You wouldn't want to ruin Garret's reputation, would you?"

"No," Jessica said quickly. "Callie's right. I don't think we should tell anyone."

"Scott wouldn't lie about this," Lindsay said again. When did she become his watchdog?

"He was joking," I pointed out. "The kid can keep a straight face no matter what. Last year he told a sub that he was allergic to chalk dust so he wouldn't have to do problems on the board!"

Jessica giggled. "That sounds like Scott."

"And he didn't crack a smile," I added. "The kid is a natural actor."

"He wasn't making it up," Lindsay said flatly. "I know Scott."

"Oh, sure you do, Lins. I know him better. So keep quiet about the bracelet." I started to walk faster, not even listening to what Lindsay was saying. The only words I caught were "know it all." I was pretty sure she was talking about me.

"Hi, ladies!" Luisa called out.

"Great party, Callie!" said MaryBeth. "Move your towel over, Luisa."

Luisa stood up and helped make room for Lindsay, Jessie, and me. As soon as I spread out my towel, MaryBeth reached up and took my wrist.

"Oh, here it is. The bracelet looks great with your tan, Callie."

"Thanks." I glanced over at Lindsay, whose whole mouth was puckered up as if she were sucking on a lemon. It was killing her that she couldn't start spilling the facts about my bracelet.

"Did Garret stay at your house for a while and talk?" I made a big production of looking for my suntan lotion in my swim bag so I wouldn't have to look at her. If she broke into a huge smile and looked dreamy, I might scream.

"No, not really." MaryBeth tapped my leg. "I think he likes you."

"What?" My head shot up.

"He does! He asked a zillion questions about you." MaryBeth grinned. "He thinks you're really nice."

"Which you are," Luisa added cheerfully.

"Yeah, sure," I said uneasily. Why would a boy ask someone as gorgeous as MaryBeth about someone as . . . as ordinary as me? I wasn't trying to feel sorry for myself, but the girl was the prettiest in our class. In any class!

"Yeah, MaryBeth struck out!" giggled Luisa.

"I wasn't trying to steal him," said MaryBeth. "I mean, once I saw the bracelet he gave you, I figured he already liked you."

Lindsay made a choking sound. I turned my back on her.

"I don't think so." But I smiled. "So, what did he say about me?"

MaryBeth laughed. "Not that you care."

"He is sooooo cute." I sat up and looked around the pool. "Is he here?"

Luisa pointed to the snack bar. "Yeah, he's here with Scott and Brad."

I glanced down at the bracelet. Would Garret think I was dumb wearing his bracelet to the pool?

Jessica tapped my back. "Callie, do you want to go get a Coke or something?"

"No!" I said it so quickly, everyone laughed. "I mean, we just got here."

"I felt funny being around Joey Lamerts when I liked him last year," confided MaryBeth. "I was always afraid I would trip, or end up with parsley stuck between my teeth."

"Oh, I know," said Luisa. "Remember when I liked Mike Anderson and I came walking out of the girls' room with a long piece of toilet paper stuck to my shoe? I could have died."

We all laughed. All except Lindsay. She was still sucking on her lemon.

"That's funny," I said. I reached in my swim bag for a scarf to tie back my hair.

"Oh, here, let me help you," offered MaryBeth. She sat up and started brushing my hair. "Can't have you looking bad in front of Garret."

"Here, use my scarf," offered Luisa. "It matches your suit. And your fab-u-lous new bracelet!"

"Gosh, thanks." I sat up straighter, trying not to smile from ear to ear. I felt so pampered. MaryBeth had always been nice, but she was paying so much attention to me, I felt great.

"Now, if I were you," advised MaryBeth, "I'd walk over and get a Coke, but pretend you don't see Garret." MaryBeth patted my hair. "You look pretty, Callie."

"I do?"

"Wait, a second," laughed Luisa. "Don't walk over to the refreshment stand, that's too obvious."

"You're right," agreed MaryBeth.

"Go over to the guard's room and ask them for a deck of cards," suggested Luisa. "Garret will see you and come to you."

MaryBeth laughed. "Yeah, very subtle, Luisa."

Luisa shined her knuckles on her shoulder. "Natch. I wrote the book on being subtle, all right."

"Oh, brother," I heard Lindsay mutter. She stood up and shoved her sunglasses up on her nose. "I'm thirsty. Want to come get a drink, Jessica?"

"What?" Jessica looked startled. "Who me?"

Lindsay nodded. "Yeah. I mean, if that's all right with you and your coaches, Callie."

"Coaches!" laughed MaryBeth. "Hey, that's good. Want Luisa and me to coach you, Callie?"

I should have spoken up right away, telling

MaryBeth that Lindsay was already my coach. I could feel Lindsay's eyes on me. She was waiting for me to say it, too.

But I didn't say a word. I just sat there and let MaryBeth and Luisa think I wanted their advice instead.

13

For the rest of the afternoon, I really did hang on every word MaryBeth and Luisa said. They were paying so much attention to me, as if the gold bracelet I was wearing added a sparkle to me that had been absent before.

" 'Bye, guys!" I called out as I gathered up my towel and headed toward the gate. "See you tomorrow."

"Thanks for nothing!" snapped Lindsay as we walked across the gravel parking lot. "First of all, you don't want me as a coach, and then you just hire two more. Make up your mind, lady."

"Lins, I want you to coach me, I really do," I insisted.

"Oh, sure." Lindsay's voice cracked. She sounded as if she were ready to cry. "Until a better offer is made."

"Lins." I put my good arm around her. "I'm sorry. I just didn't want to make a big deal out of saying that you were already my coach. It would sound silly to them. MaryBeth and Luisa were just trying to be nice to me."

"Yeah, so they could rope Garret and those boys into spending the whole afternoon playing cards on their towels." Lindsay shook back her hair. "Boy, Jessie, shoot me if I ever turn into a boy-crazy fool."

"I'm not boy-crazy!" I took back my arm.

Lindsay didn't say anything, but I saw her shoot Jessica an "oh-yes-she-is" look.

"And MaryBeth and Luisa aren't, either," I added.

Lindsay nudged Jessica. "Oh, gosh. Don't tell me I insulted Callie's new best friends. Maybe she won't let us sit with her at the pool tomorrow."

"Oh, stop it," I said. "You two are my best friends. You always will be. Aren't we the Three Musketeers?"

"Ha!" Lindsay shook her head. "We were. You had your back turned to me for at least two hours today. I had to ask you twenty times if I could pleasssssssssse borrow your suntan lotion."

"I didn't hear you, Lins."

"Of course you didn't," she said dramatically. "You were too busy gushing over Garret. 'Oh, Garret.' " Lindsay raised her voice an octave so it sounded like a cartoon lady. " 'Garret, you are soooooooo funny. I am going to laugh myself to death, you darling man, you.' "

"I never said that!" I stopped walking. "Why can't you just be happy for me, Lins?"

Lindsay kept walking. "Because you are acting phony, that's why."

"No, she isn't," insisted Jessica.

"Jessica!" Lindsay grabbed onto Jessica's arm. "You said so yourself!"

Jessica turned and gave me a horrified look. Her face flushed beet-red. "I did not!"

Lindsay turned, too, looking smug. "You said that Callie was really acting like a teenager!"

"But I didn't mean it to be bad," protested Jessica.

"I am a teenager," I said calmly. I raised my arm and smoothed back my hair. "Am I supposed to pretend to be twelve for the rest of my life?"

Lindsay looked startled. "No, I want you to act older. That was the whole reason behind this summer switch deal. But you're too different now."

"Well, sorry if I'm disappointing you both." I started walking and passed them both. "See you guys later."

"We're not disappointed." Jessica ran to catch up with me. "Want to do something later, Callie?"

I stopped and let out a long breath. Maybe thirteen was a good age to start taming my temper. Lindsay couldn't help it she was acting twelve! "Sure, how about a movie?"

"The six-thirty show isn't too crowded. Come on, Lins," called Jessica. She waved her arm to hurry her up. "Callie wants to go to a movie with us tonight!"

Lindsay was busy sucking on her lemon again, but by the time we reached the corner, she had caught up with us.

"Which movie?" she asked sullenly.

"You pick," I said generously. "And my mom has to return this really gross-looking lamp to Sears so she can probably drive both ways."

"Okay," said Jessica. " 'Bye. Call us!"

"See you, Callie," Lindsay finally called out.

As soon as I walked in the door, my mother told me that Luisa had called from the pool. Twice.

"Do you want to come over to my house and play basketball?" she asked when I called her back. I could hear screaming and laughter from the pool. "Garret has these red T-shirts he said we could borrow. He wants you to be captain of the Red Barons."

"Basketball sounds fun. Sure, when?"

"About six. My mom said we could send out for pizza. It will be so much fun."

"Tonight?"

My mom was already nodding that I could go.

"Okay, see you later, Luisa."

"Oh, and Callie, why don't you wear your hair in a French braid, like you did for school pictures. You looked so cute."

I was surprised Luisa even remembered I had worn my hair that way. "Okay."

"See ya!"

"See ya, Coach!" I laughed.

It wasn't until after I had hung up that I remembered about Jessica and Lindsay and the movie plans.

I tried calling them at Jessica's right away, but Aunt Sharon said they were both outside, squirting each other with the hose.

"Did they mention anything about a movie?" I asked.

"No," said Aunt Sharon. "We were talking about going out to dinner this evening."

"Oh," I said, wondering if I should mention Luisa's party. If I did, they would both want to come. That might be kind of rude, since Luisa only asked me. "Well, I'll talk to them later," I said. "Good-bye."

I hung up the phone and raced upstairs to take a shower.

It took ten times longer than usual to take a shower and wash my hair with my left hand tied in a bread bag. By the time I got changed, my parents were already in the car, waiting for me.

I glanced at the phone on the way out the door. Part of me thought about calling Jessica and Lindsay to see if they wanted to go to the mall with my parents, but the arrangements would take forever.

"Hurry up, Callie," my dad called from the driveway.

So I turned on the back porch light and closed the door. Jessica and Lindsay would have just as much fun going out for dinner. And I knew I would have more fun at Luisa's party than going to a movie with my cousins. Jessica and Lindsay would just have to understand.

14

Luisa lives in a small white frame house on a huge corner lot. It looks like a doll's house on the inside. Her mom stencils everything, even the oak wooden stairs leading up to the second story.

"Your mom is so cool," said Garret, admiring the stenciling in the kitchen. "I wish my mom could do stuff like this. Maybe she can come over and see it one day."

"Sure," said Mrs. Mendez. "I'm sure she's busy now with a new house, new job, and all. Moving into a new house can be a lot of work."

"It's our second move this year," said Garret. "My mom wanted a good school district."

"You'll like Sweetwater," said Mr. Mendez. "Everyone's nice."

"But nobody cooks like Mrs. Mendez," said Scott, reaching over and taking a brownie. It must have been his third.

"Mrs. M. even stenciled the birdhouse out

back," said MaryBeth. "It looks so great."

Mrs. Mendez loved all the compliments. She kept grinning and setting out more bowls of snacks and fruit.

"I plugged in the VCR on the patio," she said. "In case you kids want to watch a movie outside once it gets dark."

Garret, Scott, and Jack looked extra clean, their hair still shiny wet as if they had just taken a shower. When I walked past Garret, I could smell something like lime, although it could have been Mrs. Mendez's guacamole.

"Let's go play some ball," said Scott. He was looking right at Mr. Mendez when he said it.

"You think I'm getting too old for you, Scott?" Mr. Mendez teased. He grabbed Scott and pushed him out the door. "Come on, mister. I'll spot you five points."

"Cal, want to watch?" Garret asked me.

I blushed again at the sound of my nickname. "You go ahead," I said quickly, glancing over at Mrs. Mendez. I didn't want her to think I was on some sort of private date with Garret.

"Hey, Mom," said Luisa. "Did you see what Garret gave Callie for her birthday?"

I blushed deeper than the strawberries stenciled above the deck door. Luisa was so open about everything.

"Well, happy birthday, Callie. Let me take a

peek," said Mrs. Mendez, wiping her hands on a towel as she walked over. She took my wrist and turned it left and right. "Pretty, all right." She smiled over at Garret. "Where did you get the bracelet, Garret?"

This time Garret blushed. "At the mall," he said quickly. "Some store. I don't remember where."

I glanced down at the floor, glad Scott was out of the room, gladder still Lindsay and Jessica weren't standing next to me.

"Take the snacks outside," suggested Mrs. Mendez. "I put some cold drinks in the cooler in the garage."

"Thanks, Mom." Luisa grinned and walked out the door.

"Anything you want me to do?" asked Garret.

Mrs. Mendez smiled. "Sure. Since my big basketball star is busy, would you mind turning off the sprinker out front for me?"

"Sure." Garret headed out the door, and then grabbed my hand. Actually, my wrist.

I know walking down someone's hall and then standing on a damp front porch doesn't sound very romantic, but it was. I watched the back of Garret's head, liking how careful he was not to step on Mrs. Mendez's pink flowers when he turned off the water. I couldn't possibly imagine him sneaking into a store and stealing a bracelet. It just didn't go with the rest of him. Scott had to be teasing about the stealing.

"All set," he said, wiping off his hands on his shorts.

"Garret." I glanced down at the bracelet. Now would be the perfect time to ask where he got it. If he said, "Genicore Jewelers!" I would know right off he had bought it. You had to ring a little doorbell just to get into the store.

"What?"

"I . . ." I clamped my mouth shut. WHERE DID YOU GET MY BRACELET, GARRET? I wanted to yell.

But what if he just grinned and said, "Hey, Cal, no big deal, I stole it."

"Let's go around back with the others," I suggested. "We can keep score." I refused to act like a private detective about the bracelet. Garret gave it to me. Period!

"Sure, let's go. I want to try some of the wings. My mom works till eight tonight so I'm starving."

We stepped across the damp grass and stomped our feet on the driveway.

Just then, the Mendezes' outside porch lights came on. It was so sudden, Garret and I both jumped, then laughed.

"Instant moonlight," I giggled. I glanced up at the dark sky, wondering if the clouds were going to let the real moon shine down.

"Hey, Callie!"

I jumped again. This time I didn't laugh. My heart pounded out a menacing *thump*, *thump*, *thump* as I stared into the angry faces of Jessica and Lindsay. If looks could kill, I would have been dead.

15

"What . . . what are you guys doing here?" I was so shocked to see them, my voice sounded like I was using a megaphone.

"You said your mom could drive us to the movies tonight," snapped Lindsay. "We were dropped off at your house."

Jessie stepped closer to the yard light. "Wasn't that what we decided after the pool, Callie?"

"Well, we kind of talked about it," I began. Hadn't Aunt Sharon told them I had called? I did call!

"My mom said you called to remind us about the movie," Jessica said slowly. "So, they dropped us off since they were going to try the new Italian Olive restaurant. We tried calling back but your phone was always busy."

"What?" I said again. I could feel a trickle of sweat run down from each armpit. "My phone wasn't busy." But as soon as I said it, I remembered my mother calling lots of people to let them know their Avon orders were in.

Lindsay and Jessica exchanged looks.

"Since you didn't call back, I thought you didn't need a ride with my mom." I tried a weak smile. "Sorry about the mix up, but I even tried calling you. No answer."

"We were out back," said Jessica. "But, things were already set up to go. That's why my mom dropped us off at your house."

"I don't believe this," grumbled Lindsay. "A whole night ruined."

"I didn't ruin it," I argued. "Anyway, how did you track me down here?" I sounded mad. Maybe I really sounded trapped.

Lindsay frowned at me. "Hey, we weren't following you, Callie, if that's what you think. We went inside your house and found a sheet of paper with Luisa's name on it and a trillion hearts! It didn't take a real detective to figure out you would be here with your new friends."

I stole a look at Garret, hoping he didn't connect the hearts to himself. Boy, did Lindsay have a big mouth.

Garret shook his head. "You guys sure yell a lot."

"Oh, be quiet," grumbled Lindsay.

"Lindsay!" I took a step closer. "Garret didn't do anything."

Lindsay just rolled her eyes. "What do you want us to do? It took us forever to walk all the way over here to find out what we should do now."

"Call your parents from here," I said quickly. I wasn't their baby-sitter. "They can come and pick you up."

"They are halfway to the Italian Olive, planning to have a great time on their own and now we have to call them up and tell them we're stranded?" demanded Lindsay.

"So, now what?" asked Jessica, more quietly. She glanced back over her shoulder. "Should we go back and wait at your house, Callie? Maybe your mom can drive us home when she gets back."

"That won't be for hours!" My mom would have a million questions for me. I tapped my tennis shoe on the driveway. I really didn't want to ask Luisa if both my cousins could stay at her house for a couple of hours. She had invited me. This was strictly a seventh-grade party.

"Why don't you just walk home?" asked Garret.

"It's all locked up," announced Lindsay. "My parents thought we were going to the movie with Callie, here. Since she was the one who suggested the movies in the first place."

"I never made it definite," I said. "You should have called."

"We tried and the line was always busy," repeated Lindsay.

"Oh, brother," I muttered. "You made a mistake, that's all. I do have a life, you know. I'm not always sitting in the kitchen waiting for you guys to call me back."

"You said we could have a ride!" insisted Lindsay.

"I told Aunt Sharon I had other plans," I snapped. "I said my parents were going to the mall, not me."

The lie flew out of me like a well-aimed rubber band, stinging Lindsay and Jessica so sharply, they both stood silent.

Everyone was quiet for a second, then Jessica sat down on the bottom step.

"What are we going to do?" she asked miserably.

"Call the restaurant," suggested Garret. "Page your parents. Or walk back to Callie's."

"In other words, get lost. Boy, my parents are going to be so mad," said Lindsay. She brushed past me, then turned back and took a step closer. She studied my French braid and stared at my makeup. "You know, Callie, it's a good thing the streetlights came on. I don't think I would have recognized you tonight."

My hand flew up to my hair, pleased. But when I looked back into her face, I knew she wasn't paying me a compliment.

"So what?" I said angrily. I knew my temper was seconds away from going off. Lindsay knew exactly which buttons to press.

Jessica got up slowly. "Well, I guess we'd better go into the Mendezes' and call. Want to come in with us, Callie?"

"Hey, Garret, Callie!" Luisa waved her arm from the bottom of her driveway. "Come on. The party's back here."

"Won't you wait with us?" Jessica asked.

"If you want," I started to say.

"They're big girls," Garret said. He pulled on my arm. "Come on."

"Yeah, go on," urged Lindsay. "Don't even *think* about us, Callie."

"Well, I . . ." It was surprising how easily I was led down the driveway. Garret barely had three fingers wrapped around my wrist.

"Come on, Cal!"

Ten minutes later, I thought about checking on Lindsay and Jessica. I kept watching the deck, wondering if they would come outside.

But they didn't come out. And I didn't go in.

16

I had a great time at Luisa's house. Garret paid just enough attention to me that I felt special, but not so much that I wanted to swat him away like a whining mosquito.

"See you at the pool tomorrow, Cal!" he said at nine-fifteen when his brother came by to pick him up. He thanked the Mendezes but then he came past me again and tugged on my braid. "Take care," he had said softly.

I sighed all over again, just thinking about Garret. I felt lucky.

My smile stayed on my face until I walked into the kitchen the next morning and heard my mother on the phone with Aunt Sharon. Holy cow! The picture of Lindsay and Jessica waiting under the streetlight flashed before me! How long had they waited? Who finally picked them up?

I froze in the doorway, wondering if I could just sneak back upstairs and hide under the covers for the next ten years.

"What did I do last night?" laughed my mother, "Well, let me see. I finally returned that atrocious lamp. The lady from Sears put a discount sticker on it right away."

I leaned against the doorway. Normally, I would have slid right down on the kitchen chair, listening. My aunts and mom talk to each other a lot. It's usually pretty interesting listening material.

But not this morning. Any minute now my aunt Sharon would say, "Oh, and thanks a lot, Ellie, for ruining our dinner plans last night. The waiter was carrying our penne pasta to the table when we got a phone call from Lindsay asking us to please rescue her . . ."

I drew in a deep breath and took a step back into the dining room. What exactly had I said last night? The lie shot out of me so quickly, I wasn't quite sure. But I was positive that I had lied or twisted the truth so much that it was more lie than true. Whatever I had said made Lindsay and Jessica think that I had told Aunt Sharon that I positively, absolutely was not going to go to the movies. I scratched my head and tried to think. Did I say Luisa had already asked me over, or was I pretending that I called Jessica first . . . ?

"So, then we walked around the mall until it was time to pick up Callie." My mother reached across for her coffee and saw me standing beside the sideboard. She grinned at me.

"At Luisa Mendez's house," continued my mother, stirring in a little cream. She motioned for me to come in and sit down and eat.

"What?" My mother looked up at me. Her smile slowly slid off her face. "No, she went to the cookout around six. We dropped her off then and Jessie and Lindsay weren't here."

My mother was quiet for a long time. She even stood up and turned her back on me so she could tap a pencil up and down on the counter.

"Gosh," my mother said at last. "I feel terrible, Sharon. I don't know how a mix-up like that could have happened, and . . . well, you're being nice and I will certainly discuss this with Callie." My mother turned and motioned for me to come in again. This time she looked a little mad, as if she didn't really care if I had my breakfast or not.

Before I could even slide into my seat, my mother had hung up and was drumming her fingers up and down beside me.

"Aunt Sharon was trying to be nice, but I could tell that she's very upset. What happened last night, Callie?"

I reached for the corn cereal, then shrugged. "I'm not sure. You heard me talking to Luisa last night, Mom. The plans were made before four o'clock. I never talked to Lins or Jessie after that." I poured my milk. "I don't know why they thought I was still going to the movies."

"Aunt Sharon said it was decided at the pool.

You told them I would drive both ways."

"That's not true!" I set the milk down so hard, it sloshed over the top. I mopped it up right away before my mom could get upset over that. I wanted her on my side. "You know how confused Lins can get, Mom. I've been looking out for her for years. I'm not her guardian angel, you know."

"But you talked to Aunt Sharon," my mother pointed out.

My mother's good point stumped me for a second. I tried to make a quick recovery. "I know. I know, and I told her . . . I mean, I asked her if Lins or Jessica had mentioned the movies, and she said no. Then she mentioned a restaurant. So, so I thought that meant they didn't want to go." I stopped, swallowing hard. That wasn't exactly the truth. I hated lying to my mother, even a half lie. It was like lying to myself.

I set down my spoon and tried to sort things out. Had I mentioned Luisa's party to Aunt Sharon? No. That was part of the lie I had told Lindsay.

"So, why did Aunt Sharon drop the girls off here, Callie?"

"I don't know." I tried to take a bite, but couldn't. "I guess because I told Lins and Jessie all about that lamp you wanted to return at the mall, and they knew you wouldn't mind taking them."

My mother leaned back in her chair. "Well, I

wouldn't have, but I'm not a mind reader. They have to call and set it up."

"I know. Both of them just keep expecting me to take care of them, Mom."

I glanced up at my mother, expecting her to remind me that since I am the oldest cousin, it was my job to look out for the others, it was my responsibility and blah, blah.

But she didn't. She had believed every word I told her, buying it right away without a third degree to back it up.

"I'm going outside to weed the garden, Callie. Would you mind bringing out some garbage bags for me?"

"I can help, Mom," I said eagerly. I almost wanted a little punishment for ruining Aunt Sharon's dinner party.

"Not with your wrist, honey. Go to the pool with Lins and Jessica and play cards."

"Great!" My cousins weren't mad at me! I glanced up at the phone. I would spend so much time with them today, they would forget how rude I had been to them last night. "When did Lins call?"

My mother opened the closet and took out her gardening gloves. "Lins? She didn't call."

"She didn't?" Lindsay called me every morning, usually before nine, so we could plan our day together.

The screen door slammed and I watched my

mother walk out into the garden. I looked up at the clock again. Nine thirty-seven. I watched the second hand sweep around the circle again. And again.

I could have sat there all day watching the clock and waiting for the phone to ring. But it wouldn't.

Why would my cousins waste a call on a traitor?

17

I got dressed and threw so much energy into the weed pulling, my mother made me sit in the shade at ten-fifteen. "Callie, I don't want you pulling any more weeds with your broken wrist. Your face is as red as the barn door. Now go to the pool and cool off. Please!"

"I'm sick of the pool, Mom." I grabbed a handful of clover and shot it into the pile. "This is fun, really."

My mother laughed. "Now I know you've been in the sun too long. Go on, I'm quitting, too."

I watched as my mother dusted off her shorts and went back inside. I hated pulling weeds, never knowing when a tiny brown spider was going to zoom across my fingers. But it seemed a lot more entertaining than going to the pool and being ignored by Lindsay and Jessica. My ears burned at the thought of what they were saying about me right now.

"Callie isn't one bit nice anymore," Lindsay

would say. "The moment she turned thirteen, she started lying and acting like a phoney creep."

"She didn't even care about what she did to us last night," Jessica would tack on. "She only cares about her new friends."

My mother stuck her head out the back door. "Telephone!"

"Coming." I hurried up the steps. Maybe Lindsay and Jessica had been talking about me and decided they missed me, too.

"Hi!"

It was the library, reminding me I had three books overdue. Things were more depressing than ever.

"I'm going to the pool, Mom."

"Great. Go have some fun!" she told me. "Enjoy being thirteen."

Sure, Mom. Easier said than done. I should have pulled up a kitchen chair and detailed the crummy job I'd been doing with my teenage career so far. My wrist was broken, my two best friends and cousins hated me, and the bracelet I was wearing might have been stolen. Aside from all that, being thirteen was a real picnic.

I walked into the laundry room and grabbed my *Little Mermaid* towel. Let Lindsay see it and scribble in her little notebook till her pencil snapped in two. "Callie will never be cool," she would write down. "And her temper is getting worse everyday."

I glanced in the tiny mirror by the back door and frowned. Last night's makeup was still smudged under each eye. I looked like a giant raccoon.

I went back upstairs and changed into my suit and shorts, then washed my face. I didn't even want to look in the mirror. Had Lindsay been teasing, or had I looked so different last night at Luisa's? Things seemed to be moving so fast. How did I ever end up here?

It felt funny walking to the pool by myself. I tried to remember the last time I had walked to the community pool all alone. Maybe never. When I was younger, Lindsay and I straggled behind our moms, dropping sand buckets and water rings every four feet. We had more fun walking to the pool than being at the pool. I grinned, remembering the year Lindsay had been convinced she would melt in the blue baby pool water.

"Oh, who cares if they're mad at me," I muttered, my smile disappearing. "It isn't all my fault." Who said I had to be a perfect, wonderful, never-lose-my-temper role model for Jessica and Lindsay? It wasn't like I had anyone older telling me the right thing to do. When you thought about it, being the oldest cousin wasn't a bit fair.

I walked through the green metal gates to the pool, and stood up straighter, trying to look happy. If Lindsay and Jessica wanted to ignore me for the rest of the summer, maybe my life, let them. I could always become better friends with MaryBeth and Luisa. Cousins weren't the only best friends you could have in life.

I searched the crowd for MaryBeth and Luisa. I spotted them, laughing and playing cards with a group of kids.

I felt a prickle of regret. Playing cards with other kids going into the seventh grade was nice, but no one could be more fun, or make up zanier card rules, than Lindsay.

"Okay, dar-link cousins, who ever gets a red three of hearts has to walk over and ask the guard if he streaks his hair!" or, "If you freeze the deck with an ace, you can't unfreeze it until you have two queens in your hand, or unless you buy each player a freezer pop from the snack bar!"

That Lindsay! I grinned, then frowned. Yeah, that Lindsay! She made a big deal about my temper, but what about hers? She could be pretty nasty herself when she got mad. Somebody ought to talk to her about yelling before she thinks. "Oh, Callie, with all that cheap makeup on your mean face, I barely recognized you." Saying she didn't recognize me last night was something a mean lady in a soap opera would have said.

I stopped to get a drink at the water fountain, glancing over at the shady area. Lindsay and Jessica were both there, laughing hard as they played their silly card games. Neither one bothered to look at me. Why would they miss me when they still had each other?

I flung my mermaid towel over my shoulder and walked carefully across the yard toward MaryBeth's group. I certainly didn't want to trip and have Lindsay and Jessica fall off their towels laughing.

"Hi, everyone," I said. "Can I sit with you guys?"

"Of course." MaryBeth grinned and moved her towel. "Hi, lady. We were just talking about you."

A flash of panic raced down me. "You were?" What had I done now? Maybe Lindsay had grabbed the microphone in the snack bar and announced to everyone in Sweetwater that I had a dangerous temper and was a crummy best friend.

"Be warned!" Lindsay might have shouted. "The new, improved Callie Gaitlin is really the old, rotten, lying, stab-your-best-friend-in-the-back Callie."

"Yo-hooo, Callie!" Luisa tugged at my towel. "Wake up, dream girl. Your friend, Garret, was just here, collecting orders for the snack bar. Boy, is he nice."

I smiled. Garret *was* nice. Too bad Lindsay and Jessica couldn't give him a chance. They wanted to believe the worst in him.

I spread out my towel, resisting the urge to wave to Garret as he headed toward us. Garret grinned. He smiled at just about everyone. It must be hard being the new kid in town, wanting to make new friends fast so you wouldn't miss your old ones so much.

"I told Garret to get you some Milk Duds, Callie," said MaryBeth. "He asked what your favorite candy was."

"So attentive," giggled Luisa. "Oh, those boys from Richmond."

"Hey, ladies, Garret delivery, at your service!" Garret sat down and placed a rolled up white towel in the center. "Hi, Cal. You're just in time."

With a small flourish, Garret flipped open his towel, displaying an assortment of Milk Duds, Tootsie Roll pops, an apple, and four colored sour balls. "I trust it is to your satisfaction, medames!"

"Gosh, quite a selection," I said, reaching for a box of Milk Duds.

"How much do we owe you, sir?" asked Luisa.

"Uh, nothing."

I looked up. There was something about the "Nothing" that made me sure that "Something" was going on.

"No, really. Garret," insisted MaryBeth, taking the apple. She reached into her swim bag and tossed two quarters on the towel. "Take it, Garret. Free delivery is treat enough."

"Ladies!" laughed Garret, holding up both hands in protest. "It's my treat, really. I took care of it."

"Garret, you are too, too generous," crooned Luisa, smiling from ear to ear. "I can't let you keep doing this. You treated us yesterday, too."

He had?

Garret grabbed his towel and started to walk away. "It's my treat. I insist. Besides, I put it on my tab."

"Well, thanks," said Luisa, flashing him another smile.

His tab? Since when did the snack bar at the community pool run tabs? I had known Mr. Wisterman all my life and he was strictly a cash and carry kind of guy. He had at least five index cards taped around his concession stand stating: NO CREDIT or CASH ONLY.

I put my Milk Duds down, trying hard to swallow the lump stuck in my throat. "*What* tab, Garret?"

I looked up, waiting for him to say, "So I paid cash, it's no big deal."

"My tab." Garret gave me a crooked grin. "Relax, Cal. I took care of it — I've got my ways."

I almost smiled back. But I felt a prickling on the back of my neck. I could feel my cheeks heating up and my chin rising up a notch. How stupid did Garret think I was?

As I watched Garret walk away, my fingers tightened around my bracelet. It suddenly felt heavier than the cast I wore on the other wrist.

"Luisa, can you help me with this?" I held my wrist out across her towel.

Luisa sat up and examined the clasp. "It's okay, Callie."

"No, I mean, take it off."

"What?" MaryBeth shook her head. "You'll lose it, Callie. Keep it on."

"I want it off," I said quickly. Luisa dropped it into my hand and I scrambled to my feet, hurrying before I lost my nerve. If Garret had stayed another minute, I probably would have lost my temper, too.

"Garret!" I caught up with him by the lifeguard's room.

Garret turned and smiled. "Hey, what's up?"

I took his hand and dropped the bracelet in it. "I don't think I can keep this anymore."

Garret's face reddened as he opened his palm. "What?" He glanced over at the kids playing cards and pulled me closer to the water fountains. "Scott told you, didn't he?" His voice was angry. "He's a jerk for telling."

I shrugged and took a step back as Garret held out the bracelet.

"Take it. I want you to have it, Cal."

I shook my head. "No."

Garret didn't say anything for a minute or two. "Why?"

I stood there, the sun beating down on the back of my legs, wondering how I could possibly explain everything to Garret when I was still trying to figure it out myself.

"Just tell me why," Garret asked again.

"It doesn't fit me anymore," I said quietly.

"Oh, jeez," muttered Garret. "That makes absolutely no sense at all."

I turned and started to walk away.

"Thanks for nothing, Gaitlin!" Garret called after me. "Hey, give me a call if you ever decide to grow up!" I didn't turn around, but heard coins clatter and saw a quarter and two nickels roll crazily past me.

A few kids started to laugh, others looked up and stared at me. "Grow up?" I felt like screaming. "You better be glad I have, buddy, or you'd be *swallowing* that bracelet right now."

I hurried past the concession stand, glad my dark glasses hid most of my face. I was halfway across the gravel parking lot when I heard running behind me.

I bit my lip, praying it wasn't Garret. I didn't want to make a big production out of this, and I wasn't trying to embarrass him or act like some sort of a saint.

I just wanted to be me again.

"Callie, wait!"

I spun around. Lindsay and Jessica were racing across the parking lot, their towels flying out behind them like capes.

"Holy cow!" cried Lindsay. She skidded to a stop and grinned up at me. "Talk about drama, Callie. That was better than some of my movies."

"I wasn't trying to . . ."

Lindsay slung her arm around me. "I mean, I was waiting for the director to yell *CUT!*"

"Are you okay?" Jessica asked.

I nodded, then shook my head. "I don't know. I'm okay. I'll probably be the biggest seventh-grade outcast at the junior high, but aside from that, I'm fine." I looked down. "Sorry about last night. I guess most of it was my fault."

"Ninety-nine percent," agreed Lindsay. "But who's counting, dar-link?"

Jessica patted me on the back. "We still love you, kiddo."

I nodded, not really trusting my voice just then. That's the great thing about cousins. You have so many great times with them, they're willing to overlook the not-so-great times.

Lindsay picked up my right hand. "Hmmmm-mmm, is it my imagination, or is something missing here?"

Jessica laughed. "Not that we were spying on you or anything."

"The whole pool was," confided Lindsay. "Especially when Garret threw the bracelet in the pool."

"He did?"

Lindsay grinned. "Right after he threw the money at you."

"Everyone started diving for it," added Jessica. "Except *us*, of course."

Lindsay nudged me in the side. "Yeah, your cousins are much, much too subtle for that."

"Of course," I agreed. "Nothing too subtle about me. I probably looked like a real idiot back there."

Lindsay took off her sunglasses and narrowed one eye. "I don't know. What do you think, Jessica?"

Jessica stepped back and crossed her arms. "Nah."

"Nah," laughed Lindsay. "You looked pretty good to us."

"Thanks. You two are the best mirror a girl could have."

"Hey — what's a cousin for?" asked Lindsay.

I smiled. "We better get going. I don't feel like talking to anyone else right now."

"Let's roll," laughed Jessica.

"We'll talk to the press later," agreed Lindsay. "And if they want to make this whole thing into a movie, I get to pick the girl who plays me."

"You can play yourself," I laughed. "No one else could possibly do you justice."

Lindsay flipped her long blonde ponytail back, and batted her eyes. "You are so terrrrrribly right."

"Shall we go?" I asked.

"But, of course," agreed Jessica.

Then the three of us linked arms and walked slowly up the hill and straight into the sunset, just like in Lindsay's corny old movies.

About the Author

Colleen O'Shaughnessy McKenna began her writing career as a child, when she sent off a script for the *Bonanza* series. McKenna is best known for her popular Murphy series, the inspiration for which comes from her own family.

A former elementary school teacher, Ms. McKenna lives in Pittsburgh, Pennsylvania, with her husband and four children.